FROM DAMSEL IN DISTRESS TO WARRIOR

Princess

From Damsel in Distress to Warrior Princess

ISBN: (paperback)
          (ebook)

Printed in the United States of America

FROM DAMSEL IN DISTRESS TO WARRIOR

Princess

BOOK 3 OF
THE WARRIOR QUEEN AND
KING OF THE ROAD
TRILOGY

FLYING CARMAN

DEDICATION

To Oksanka, a Russian lady that God made for me

CHAPTER 1

IT WAS THE BEGINNING OF October in Covington, GA and the Crystal triplets, Barda, Dinah, and Kara, were settling in, along with all the other students, to their seats in homeroom. This was the beginning of senior year for the triplets, and soon they'd be graduating. They couldn't wait for the time when they could just wake up and go to help their parents, Tori and Ted, and their family-owned and family-operated business, CRYSTAL CLASSICS AND CUSTOMS. There was nothing more that the triplets loved than getting into the shop and helping detail, restore, or customize a car, except racing on their private drag strip at home, OLD MUSCLE FARM, or training at their mom's martial arts dojo.

Their training was something Barda, Dinah, and Kara tried to keep to themselves, since they and their mom were descendants of the Greek Warrior Queen, Xena. Their mom, Tori, whose name was actually short for Torino (as in Ford Gran Torino), was the modern era Warrior Queen, and had told her daughters that Xena herself had appeared to her and Ted and awarded her the title. So, over the course of their childhood, the triplets had endured grueling trials, and had succeeded in earning their Warrior Princess titles. Little did they know that this year, they all would be put to the ultimate test.

The triplets, along with all their classmates were quietly talking amongst each other when their teacher, Mrs. Bailey called the class to order.

"Class," she announced, "we have a real treat this year: we get to welcome two foreign exchange students from Russia, who also happen to be sisters; come in, ladies." After a couple seconds, two very pretty girls entered the room. They were also a little on the tall side, even though they weren't wearing high heels, and appeared a bit fierce and a bit shy at the same time. One had reddish-brown hair and eyes that seemed somewhere between a bright sapphire and a bright aquamarine, while the other had bright blond hair and pale green eyes. However, the Crystal triplets noticed that the two foreign sisters seemed to be constantly watching them with desperate, pleading eyes, as if they were silently crying out "***Please, help us***". Mrs. Bailey introduced them as Dominika, the blue-eyed brunette, and Marta, the green-eyed blond, Borov from Moscow, Russia.

"Please make them feel welcome, everyone," Mrs. Bailey continued, "you ladies can sit back by the Crystal triplets." She directed the two Russian girls to a pair of empty desks near where the Crystals were sitting. Once the Borovs were seated, Mrs. Bailey got their lesson on World History on Ancient Greece started. As the class went on, the Crystals couldn't help noticing the Borovs continued to watch them with those same pleading looks on their pretty faces. Plus, Barda, Dinah, and Kara could feel the plea, not just see it.

After ninety minutes of learning Greek myths and legends, the bell rang. Dinah had art class next, Barda was off to P.E., and Kara had creative writing. As the triplets were heading for the door, they noticed that the Borovs were quietly following them. Since they'd been raised to be neighborly, the Crystals stopped and asked the two Russian sisters if they needed help finding their next class. Marta said she had art class and Dominika said she had creative writing next, so Dinah and Kara were more than willing to show the new girls to their next class.

As Kara walked with Dominika, she noticed that the Russian girl looked calmer and more relaxed, as if she felt safer. *That's strange,* Kara thought, *how could being with me make her happier and calmer?* Meanwhile, Dinah was thinking the same thing as she escorted Marta to art class. Upon arrival, the art teacher, Mrs. Renner, assigned Marta to the same table as Dinah. When they got started with their drawing assignment, Dinah noticed that Marta was a phenomenal artist.

"That's really incredible work, Marta," Dinah whispered.

"Thank you, Dinah," the Russian girl whispered back, "my sister and I have always been creative, me with pictures and Dominika with words." Dinah was surprised by how good her English was, but she did know that a lot of Russians could speak English. Meanwhile, in Mr. Sandler's creative writing class, Kara had noticed that Dominika had very beautiful scripted handwriting.

"Were you taught that or did you make it up yourself," she asked, "I don't think I could ever write like that."

"It's a gift, Kara," Dominika answered softly, "I'm a talented writer."

"Have you written books or anything, Dominika?"

"Stories, but never published, Kara."

"Nice." Kara was awed by her new friend, and Dominika seemed to be able to tell that Kara thought of her as a friend, for she smiled a very dazzling smile that, Kara was positive, would make any guy want to follow her. Back in the art room, Dinah and Marta had become fast friends also, and it seemed that Marta's smile was just as bright as her sister's. However, Dinah and Kara did notice that the two Russian girls seemed desperate, as if they were trying to run and hide from something or someone.

Eventually, it was lunch time and Barda, Dinah, and Kara found their usual lunch table and began their usual lunch time chatter. No sooner had they begun, the Borov sisters walked up and asked if they could join the Crystals at their table. Since they'd already gotten to know the two Russian girls a bit, the triplets agreed. Over the course of the lunch period, the Crystals and the Borovs got to know each other more, but it was Dinah who had to ask the question that Barda and Kara seemed to be avoiding.

"Why do you two seem so fascinated by us," she asked, "you always seem to be watching us."

"Yeah," Barda agreed, "and why do you always seem to have these pleading looks in your eyes all the time?" When she said this, Marta and Dominika looked a bit startled, like they'd just been caught stealing cookies in the middle of the night. However, after a few seconds, Dominika broke the awkward quiet.

"Caught that, huh," she whispered.

"It *is* quite obvious, you two," Kara replied, "are the two of you hiding something?" This question took a bit for an answer, but eventually, Marta talked a little.

"We kind of are," she responded, very quietly, "but don't worry, it's nothing illegal or anything like that."

"Then what is it," Dinah asked. The two Russian sisters looked at each other, and both of them answered.

"We can't tell you here," they quietly replied, "however, we *want* to tell you." Then, trying to break the awkwardness, Dominika spoke up.

"You three are the most beautiful girls here, not to mention the nicest; not everyone we've met in our lives has been beautiful and nice, or even come close to your level of kindness."

"Agreed, sis," Marta chimed in. Though the Crystals accepted the complements, they were still confused. However, the bell rang before they could ask any further questions.

The afternoon sped by pretty quick, with Barda getting to know the two Russian girls better in her mythology class she shared with Dominika, as well as her graphic design class she shared with Marta. Finally, when school let out, the Crystals headed out to the far corner of the parking lot where they'd left their muscle cars. Once they got there, they happened to notice the Borovs being picked up by a nasty looking man in a black 1997 Lincoln Town Car. Though it was strange, the triplets decided to discuss it with their parents once they got back to the farm.

After arriving back home about fifteen minutes later, they stashed their cars, Big Red (1970 Chevrolet Chevelle SS), Big Boss (1970 Ford Boss 302 Mustang), and Triple Bird (1970 Plymouth Road Runner) in the barn and brought their packs in and told their parents about their new friends. Tori and Ted were happy that their daughters had made the foreign girls feel welcome, yet they too were confused when the triplets told of how Marta and Dominika kept looking at them with pleading eyes. They also were confused when their daughters told them about the mean looking man who picked them up after school.

"I'd say just keep being the way y'all were today with them," Ted told them, "I feel that once they feel safe and OK with being around you three, they may open up."

"I think they have more than they're willing to tell right now," Tori added, "I suggest you girls continue, like your father said, being the way you are when you're with them; who knows, maybe they need some love and comfort." Barda, Dinah, and Kara didn't yet realize how right their mother was.

CHAPTER 2

When Marta and Dominika were dropped off at their little flat that the city had provided for them, they quickly unpacked and got their homework done. It wasn't until Marta started making a small, simple dinner for the two of them that they started talking.

"I *really* hope we can gain our freedom here, Marta," Dominika told her sister with a shudder, "you know what'll happen to us if we can't."

"I know, Domi," Marta replied, "and I know, and you know, that the Crystals can help us, but we can't tell them just yet; it's too early."

"Yes, but I get the sense that they suspect something is up with us."

"Probably because we've been watching them with pleading looks on our faces; we need to act more casual, Dominika, though it's amazing how you've been so calm, what with that ability of yours." What nobody knew, anyone outside of the Borov family at least, was that Dominika had been born with synesthesia, the ability to basically read minds, just like Dominika Egorova in the **RED SPARROW** book trilogy by ex-CIA agent Jason Matthews.

"Plus," Marta went on, "we need to be extra careful about that Mr. Blohkin; I have a feeling he was sent by the Russian government to watch us and make sure we don't try to accomplish what we came to do."

"Agreed," Dominika sighed, "I have a feeling if he hears any of our conversations, we'll either be dead or shipped off to State School Four faster than we can spell both of our names; and THAT is what scares me." At this, she shuddered hard, but her sister turned from the stove and rubbed her sister's hand. Marta then got their dinner served and they ate in silence.

Once the sisters had finished and cleaned up the kitchen, they quickly showered and dressed for bed. Their flat was basically a small, two-story, three bedroom, two-and-a-half bath cottage with the kitchen, living, and dining rooms on the main floor with a small powder room and the three bedrooms and two main bathrooms on the second floor. Marta fell asleep rather quickly, but Dominika stayed awake for a while, thinking. She felt that she had a deep connection with the Crystals, for she seemed to sense that she'd always known them. It was like, in another life, she'd been a part of their family. *It seems so strange,* she thought, *I'm Russian born, and a bit Russian stubborn, but I seem to be connected to an American family; what does it mean?*

Over the course of the night, both of the Borovs recalled their mother's dying wish: that they flee from Russia and go to America before the State forced them into State School Four aka Sparrow School. Their mother told them that if they got sent there, they'd basically be forced to become government prostitutes, aka Sparrows, who were forced to have sex with government agents from other countries to coax top secret information out of them, the ancient art of 'sexpionage'. When she'd found out that this was what the government wanted to do to her daughters, she quickly contacted a friend of hers, Daria, who worked with foreign affairs in America. Daria immediately had gotten the approvals for Mrs. Borov's girls to travel to America, but they'd only just barely escaped out of Russia, for Russian government agents had come to collect Dominika and Marta shortly after their mother drew her last breath. When Vladimir Putin heard that the Borov sisters had escaped the country, naturally he was furious and dispatched Vantov Blohkin, a government official, to keep an eye on them. Blohkin's orders were to find out where the sisters were living and rig up hidden cameras and microphones to listen in on their activities. If any talk of defection was heard, he was ordered to kill the sisters or drag them back to Russia for immediate admission to Sparrow School. Of course, Blohkin wasn't staying in Covington. He rented a room in a motel near the highway, so that he wouldn't draw attention to himself. Every night, he'd listen to the recordings and watch the footage from the Borov's flat. As he did this, it seemed that they were thinking of defecting, but he couldn't be one hundred percent sure just yet. So, he decided to wait a few days to see if any solid evidence along those lines came up.

The next day at school, the Crystals noticed that the Borovs seemed more nervous and desperate looking then they'd been yesterday. However, they did what their parents told them to do, and kept trying to help Marta and Dominika adjust to the school. Yet, when they all sat down at lunch, Barda, Dinah, and Kara all noticed how Marta and Dominika seemed very twitchy, and that their beautiful eyes kept flicking around the room. What really seemed to brighten up the two Russian girls was when Dinah suggested that the Borovs come to the farm after school for a study session, which Marta and Dominika quickly, and excitedly, agreed to.

"Thank you very much," Marta gushed, small happy tears coming out of her eyes.

"Yes, many thanks indeed," Dominika said, nearly in a squeal.

"Settled then," Kara proclaimed, "we'll meet you guys by the front doors and walk to our cars." Just as they agreed on it, the bell rang.

Dominika and Kara headed to their U.S. History class, Barda headed for P.E., and Dinah and Marta set off for Geometry.

Two hours later, the Borovs met the Crystals by their lockers instead of the front doors. Barda, Dinah, and Kara found it a bit odd, but didn't say anything. Once outside, the Crystals noticed that their Russian friends were constantly looking around. Barda, Dinah, and Kara didn't quite understand this either, but what Marta and Dominika were doing was watching for Blohkin and his black Lincoln. However, he didn't show up until after the Borovs and the Crystals were in their cars. Marta chose to ride with Dinah and Dominika rode with Kara, but they both ducked out of sight when Blohkin and his Lincoln showed up. Both Dinah and Kara asked what they were ducking down for, and the two Russian girls said they didn't want Blohkin to see them. Dinah and Kara both felt that it was weird, but when they saw how mean Blohkin looked, they silently agreed with the Borovs. Once off the school grounds, and making sure that Blohkin wasn't following them, the Crystals drove toward home.

When Old Muscle Farm came into view, Marta and Dominika were awestruck at how beautiful it was. The two Russian sisters were even more amazed when their friends drove into the barn and beheld the enormous car collection that they had, especially the exotic Ferraris and Lamborghinis, as well as the seven Bugattis. Once the Crystals got their cars parked in their stalls, they walked their friends over to the house and introduced them to Ted and Tori.

"It's a pleasure to meet both of you," Ted told them, "the triplets have told us a lot about you two."

"I'm glad that our girls are making you two feel welcome," Tori added, "as well as helping you adjust to life here."

"Thank you very much," the Borovs both answered, then looked at each other and blushed. Ted told them not to be embarrassed, that Barda, Dinah, and Kara had done that same thing also.

"Your place is very lovely, Mr. and Mrs. Crystal," Dominika said.

"Thank you, Dominika," Tori replied, "that's very kind of you to say."

"We were taught to always be polite," Marta chimed in before adding, "does everyone in America have more than one car?"

"That depends on how much money you make and how well you manage that money," Ted answered, "it also depends on what kind of car you want and if you have the space." After some more light chatter, the girls retreated to the living room to work on their homework and to study some. The Crystal triplets helped the Borov sisters as much as possible, which Marta and Dominika found extremely comforting, and the two even shared with Barda, Dinah, and Kara a little about growing up in Russia. The triplets were amazed that their friends' mother, Irina, had been a famous Russian singer.

"We even have all of her CDs and some of her costumes she wore with us at our little flat," Marta explained, "she had an absolutely incredible voice."

"What about your father," Kara asked.

"Sadly he died when we were only four," Dominika answered, "his name was Peter and from what mother told us, he was a poet; that is what attracted mother to him."

"And he loved mother very much," Marta added.

"That's sad," Barda said, and she and her sisters hugged their friends.

"Thank you," the Borovs said together, blushing. At that, they continued on with their homework.

At around 4:00, Tori announced that dinner was ready. The Crystal triplets and their foreign friends came back to the kitchen for a lovely dinner of homemade meatloaf and baked sweet potatoes, which Marta and Dominika found quite good. Dessert was some lovely homemade brownies and milk. Once dinner was over, and the dishes were cleared, Kara volunteered to drive the Borovs back to their flat.

After Marta and Dominika got back to their flat, they bid farewell and thank you to Kara and once she and Big Boss were out of sight, they headed inside. The two Russian girls quickly showered and headed for bed, but they couldn't fall asleep immediately, even though they were tired.

"I'm worried, Dominika," Marta whispered, "if Blohkin is watching us, he'll no doubt be extremely angry that we weren't at school when he came to fetch us today."

"Agreed," Dominika whispered back, "I *know* we need to tell the Crystals we need their help, and we'd better be quick about it."

"Yes, but we need to tell them where no unfriendly ears are listening."

"I say after school on Friday, Marta, agreed"

"Agreed." Once that was said, Marta and Dominika dropped off to sleep. Back in his hotel room, Blohkin was indeed angry that the Borovs hadn't been at school when he'd come to pick them up and hadn't come back to their flat until after sunset. Therefore, he decided to act upon his orders, and he decided to do so that Friday, after he picked them up at school, a little earlier then usual dismissal.

CHAPTER 3

On Friday, Blohkin came to the school and told the officials that Marta and Dominika had an emergency at their flat and had to leave early to take care of it. This was, of course, a lie he'd cooked up, but the officials believed him, so the two Russian girls were sent off with him in his Lincoln. When they arrived at the flat, Blohkin told them he needed to come in and use the bathroom. Marta and Dominika both did their best to hide their panic, but their facades broke as soon as he was inside the hall powder room. Marta went into the kitchen to gather some food while Dominika raced upstairs to gather their personal possessions. Fortunately, the number of personal items the sisters had wasn't much, so it didn't take Dominika long to round it all up and stuff it into her backpack, including their mother's costumes and her CDs. Taking the far stairway back down, she heard a commotion coming from the kitchen. As Dominika approached the kitchen, she heard Marta gasping for breath, and Blohkin's sinister voice.

"You two have been very naughty," he growled, "and now you're going to pay the price." She poked around the corner of the wall and saw that Blohkin had her sister in a tight grip and a sharp knife in one hand. Blohkin was watching Marta and he saw her eyes move toward the kitchen entrance and he saw Dominika standing there, frozen in horror.

"I'll make sure your admittance to State School Four is quick and fast, Dominika Borov," Blohkin snarled, "I'm very sure you'll make an excellent little Sparrow."

"Let my sister go," Dominika yelled, despite her fear.

"Forget about me, Dominika, and save yourself," Marta gasped.

"I can't abandon you, Marta."

"Go, sister," Marta croaked, just as Blohkin slashed the knife across her throat, sending blood flying, some splattering on Dominika's clean white shirt.

"*NO*," Dominika screamed as Blohkin dropped her sister's dead body to the floor. He made a lunge for her, but she dodged the attack and kicked out at Blohkin's side with everything she had, sending him crashing into a table beside the living room wall. As Blohkin lay there groaning, Dominika raced out the door. Now, she and her sister had purchased two bicycles shortly after they'd arrived in America and had been keeping them close to the front door. Once Dominika was outside, she jumped onto her bike and raced off as fast as she could pedal.

As she raced away, Dominika could feel hot tears coming into her eyes, but she quickly brushed them away, since she had to concentrate on where she was heading. Plus, she knew that even though she had a head start, she wouldn't be able to outrun Blohkin and his Lincoln. Just as the Russian girl was thinking this, she glanced behind her and saw that Blohkin and his Lincoln were coming up on her. Determined, she turned back forward and kept pedaling. Suddenly, she heard gunfire, and realized with horror that he was either going to run her down, or shoot her!

Just as the woods came into view ahead, Dominika felt that the sharp sting of a bullet grazing her left calf. She faltered a bit, but somehow managed to stay upright, and raced into the woods where

Blohkin's car couldn't follow. As she disappeared among the trees, Blohkin brought his Lincoln to a halt and climbed out.

"Oh well, she'll die soon from shock and blood loss," he muttered to himself, "right now, I'll get back to the flat and alert the boys to come and collect her sister's body for immediate return to Russia." With that, he got back in his car and headed back to the flat. Meanwhile, Dominika was still pedaling, but she was growing weak. All of a sudden, her front tire hit a rock and catapulted her headfirst into a rock in a shallow pond, knocking her out cold.

After what seemed like forever, Dominika came to. She immediately began to shiver, since she was soaked through. Slowly, she lifted a hand to her head and was scared when it came away wet and very red. As quickly as she could in her weakened state, the Russian girl crawled out of the pond and further into the woods. A little while later, she was still crawling and her vision was going in and out of focus, but she could feel a paved path, and heard water and birds. Dominika had found herself beside the fishing lake in the main park. Also, she happened to see a car parked nearby that she recognized, the General Lee. She remembered the General from when the Crystals had invited her and Marta to their farm for a study session, so she knew they had to be nearby, but she also knew they couldn't find her like this just yet. As quickly and quietly as she could, she made her way over to the old Charger, climbed into the trunk, and covered herself with a blanket.

A minute later, she heard the voices of Barda, Dinah, and Kara. Although she was overjoyed, Dominika knew she had to keep quiet, which she thought would be difficult, for she was shivering hard. The injured Russian girl heard her friends load another blanket and a basket into the trunk and close the lid. Then, she felt the engine start and the car begin to move. At the same time, the Crystals were happily chatting about their picnic.

"I gotta say, Dinah," Barda began, "you really know how to make a picnic fun."

"Yeah," Kara chimed in, "the biscuits you made were the best."

"Thanks guys," Dinah answered from the driver's seat, blushing a bit, "were we hearing gun shots a little bit ago?" Barda and Kara did remember hearing what sounded like gun fire before they'd packed up.

"I don't know, maybe," Kara replied, "I do believe hunting season has started."

"Still, I think it is a bit odd that it was heard in the daytime," Barda added. However, they brushed it off and continued on their trek back to the farm. When the triplets got back and had parked the General in his stall in the barn Kara, who was getting out of the back, thought she heard a rattle coming from the trunk.

"Sisters," she said, "I think there is something alive in the General's trunk." So Kara and her sisters came around to the back of the Charger, and sure enough, heard a rattle coming from inside the trunk. Opening the trunk, the rattle sounded like it was coming from under one of the blankets. Dinah moved the blanket, and all three were horrified at what they found underneath.

"*DOMINIKA*," the triplets gasped at the same time. Their foreign friend was deathly pale, completely soaked, covered in blood, dirt, and forest debris, and heavily, uncontrollably shivering. Plus, they noticed what turned out to be frozen tears stuck to her beautiful face. She slowly looked up at her friends with slightly glazed eyes and tried not to slur her words as she spoke up.

"*P-p-pomogi m-m-mne*," she quietly begged, but upon seeing their confused expressions, switched to English and repeated her plea, "h-h-help m-m-me!" At that, Barda and Kara quickly but gently got her out of the General's trunk while Dinah quickly made a CB call over to the house to get their parents. When Ted and Tori got to the barn, they also were horrified upon seeing Dominika, but they quickly shoved that aside as they helped their daughters get their friend to the house.

Once in the house, the Crystals carried Dominika to the downstairs bathroom, which had a full soaker tub and got the hot water on. As they waited for the tub to fill, Barda and Dinah took Dominika's backpack off and then slowly peeled off her dripping wet clothes. When the tub had gotten to a good level, they, all five, slowly and carefully lowered Dominika into the tub and began to clean her up, hoping to get all the blood off, and that the warm water would warm her up also. When they felt they'd gotten all the blood and dirt off, Ted and Barda carefully lifted Dominika out of the tub and Tori, Dinah, and Kara quickly wrapped her in towels and they all carried her upstairs to the guestroom.

Once the Russian girl was laid on the bed Kara, the healer, used her 'special gift' to heal Dominika's wounds. They all then quickly got her under the heavy quilt and tucked in. However, everyone noticed that she was still very pale and couldn't seem to stop shivering. Yet, they thought that some time under the covers would calm her and warm her up.

About a half hour later, Ted came back to the room to check on her, and he was scared when he saw his daughters' friend. Dominika was still pale and shivering. Though he quickly collected himself and asked her how she was doing.

"I-I-I'm f-f-fine, M-M-Mr. C-C-Crystal," Dominika answered in between shivers. Ted then felt his guest's head, hands and feet, and was shocked. They were still ice cold! He knew that if Dominika didn't get warm, and fast, she'd exhaust her strength from trying to fight the hypothermia. Thinking quickly, and remembering something he'd read in a book, he started a fire in the fireplace and came back over to the bed.

"Would it be alright if I laid with you, Dominika, to help warm you up," he asked. Dominika was a little shocked and surprised, since she was totally naked. Yet, upon seeing the kindness in his eyes, and his thoughts, she nodded. Ted then removed his shirt, shoes, and socks, got under the blankets, and gently nestled Dominika as close to him as he could, willing his body heat to warm her.

Since she was still shivering, Dominika found herself whimpering, but once Ted had nestled her close to him, he quietly assured her she'd be alright. She'd covered her large breasts with her hands, but when her host began to try to warm her up, he wrapped his arms around her waist. The Russian girl felt strangely like she was at home as Ted's body heat, and the heat from the fire in the fireplace began to warm her freezing body. When she heard Ted start to softly hum to her, she was shocked to find herself snuggling closer, just like she had when she was a little girl and her father used to lie with her on cold evenings in their little apartment just outside Moscow. Soon, she actually drifted off to sleep.

When the clock chimed four, Ted quietly roused his young guest. Upon waking, Dominika was a bit disoriented, since she remembered not waking up in this room at the beginning of the day. However, she remembered how her friend's father had laid with her to help get her warm after her terrible ordeal. She sat up, trying to keep her breasts covered, and saw him just finishing pulling his shirt back on. Looking out the window, she was surprised to see it was nearly twilight. So, she figured she'd better speak up.

"I thank you kindly, Mr. Crystal," she told him quietly, "I owe you, and your daughters, my life."

"Ahh, glad we could help, Dominika," Ted answered with a kind smile, "I know that Barda, Dinah, and Kara are going to be happy you're alright."

"Yes, I'm sure," the Russian girl responded, "I love your daughters; you and Mrs. Crystal definitely raised them right."

"Thanks, I'll pass that along; I'm heading downstairs to join the family for dinner; would you like me to bring you up some food?"

"What are you having?"

"Tuna burgers and salmon fillets."

"Probably just a salmon fillet would be nice."

"Okay, I'll be back in a little bit." With that, Ted headed downstairs to join Tori and the triplets. He told them that Dominika had warmed up and that she was doing well.

"Is she joining us, Honey," Tori asked.

"I'll take her up a fillet and some milk," Ted replied, "I think she should rest." As the family ate, they kept wondering why and how Dominika had headed up in the trunk of the General Lee the way she had this afternoon. Once the family had their share, Ted took up a salmon fillet and some cool milk for Dominika. When he entered the guest room, she was sleeping quietly. Ted couldn't help but admire how this young Russian girl seemed so peaceful right now, but seemed totally terrified when she was awake. He gently whispered her name and Dominika awoke.

"I have dinner for you, Dominika," he told her, sitting the tray on her lap. As she sat up, her breasts started to get exposed again, and she tried vainly to cover them. Ted laughed softly and removed his shirt and handed it to her.

"Throw this on, Honey," he told her, "at least then you'll be able to eat and not have to worry about being exposed." Dominika giggled a little, but accepted the shirt.

"It isn't like you haven't already seen, and felt, my breasts, Mr. Crystal," she said. After throwing Ted's shirt on, she ate. She thoroughly enjoyed the fish and the milk was perfect to go with it.

"I'll let Tori know, Dominika," Ted told her, "we're all going to sleep soon, but Tori and I are right across the hall if you need anything."

"Thank you, Mr. Crystal."

An hour later, the lights at Old Muscle Farm were off, except for the outside lights. Ted and Tori were settling in for the night and had Dominika on their minds.

"How did she end up in the General's trunk with a head wound and a calf wound, Honey," Tori wondered out loud.

"I dunno," Ted answered, "but we should ask her in the morning." Just as they were about to doze off, they heard a scream coming from the guestroom. Tori and Ted bolted over there, though they saw that their daughters had gotten there first, somehow. Dominika had the covers twisted around her and she was almost in hysterics, for it sounded nearly like she was being tortured. Fortunately, Tori and Kara got the Russian girl to wake up, and once she saw that her friends were around her, she quickly calmed down.

Upon collecting herself, Dominika knew that now was the time. It was time for her to tell the Crystals, who she literally saw as her new family, why she and Marta had actually come to America in the first place.

CHAPTER 4

"I NEED TO TELL YOU all this," Dominika began slowly, "Marta and I aren't foreign exchange students; we're actually trying to defect."

"You are," Tori exclaimed, "why?"

"Our parents died before we came here, Mrs. Crystal," Dominika explained, "on her death bed, mother told Marta and I that she was sending us to America because the government back home intended to ship us off to State School Four once we turned eighteen."

"You were going to be forced to become Sparrows," Ted burst out, nearly in a yell of anger, yet he quickly collected himself.

"How do you know that, Mr. Crystal?"

"I'll tell you later; continue with your story." Dominika then basically told the Crystals her life story, and that her father had died during a riot. The government sent their "condolences", yet Dominika and her family knew it was just hogwash. Then, she explained how her mother had legally made the arrangements to send her daughters to America to escape their fate. Everything had gotten approved, but somehow Russian agents found out, and Marta and Dominika just barely made it out of Russia. She also explained about Blohkin and how he'd been sent to "watch over and protect them", but she and Marta knew that he was an agent for the Russian government sent to keep tabs on them. However, the Crystals noticed that when their foreign friend got to the events of the day, she started to lose her composure.

"Dominika," Kara asked, "why wasn't Marta with you when we found you?"

"When Blohkin dropped us at out flat, he said he needed to come inside," Dominika explained, "Marta and I realized that he sensed something was up; she'd gone into the kitchen to gather some food for our escape, but Blohkin caught her before we could get out."

"Where were you," Dinah asked.

"I'd gone upstairs to gather our personal things, which are still in my backpack," the Russian girl replied, desperately fighting to hold back her tears, "when I got back downstairs, Blohkin was dragging her out of the kitchen by her neck."

"Then…," Barda pressed.

"Marta told me to leave her and save myself," Dominika continued, appearing to be getting more sad with each passing second, "but I couldn't abandon the only family I had left."

"Understandable," Ted murmured, "carry on."

"Blohkin told me that I'd be an excellent Sparrow, and that Marta and I had been very naughty and had to pay for it; then he… he.."

"What," the Crystals asked all at once.

Dominika couldn't hold back her anguish any longer and it just exploded out of her very heavily, causing her to drop the blanket covering her body.

"HE SLIT HER THROAT RIGHT IN FRONT OF ME," she wailed shrilly, as the tears burst out of her beautiful sapphire / aquamarine eyes and the sobs burst from her throat. This single statement caused *everyone* to cry, for the Crystals formed a circle around Dominika and hugged her, being careful not to bump or touch her breasts so she wouldn't freak out more, and quietly wept for her, for Marta, and for Dominika's parents.

After five minutes, and two whole boxes of tissues, the circle backed up, though Dominika didn't pull the blanket back over herself, to her own surprise as much as the surprise of the Crystals. Kara then asked Dominika how she'd ended up in the trunk of the General Lee.

"After Blohkin killed my sister," Dominika began, still sniffling a bit, "he lunged at me, but I dodged it and kicked him into a corner, which knocked him silly for a bit; I ran outside, got on my bicycle and took off."

"Did he chase you at all," Tori asked.

"Yes, in that black Lincoln of his, and he shot at me; that was the wound on my calf, though the bullet only grazed my calf."

"So we *did* hear gun shots this afternoon," Dinah exclaimed.

"Yes; he gave up the chase when I got into the woods, but my bike hit a rock and I got flung into a pond and hit my head on a rock."

"That's why you were all wet then, huh," Barda asked.

"Yes; once I'd regained my senses, I crawled out of the pond and eventually found the General; I climbed into its trunk and covered myself," Dominika finished, "you all know the rest." Ted and Tori told the triplets that they should head off to bed, since there was going to be a heap of chores in the morning. Barda, Dinah, and Kara left, each of them giving Dominika a kiss before leaving. Once the triplets were out of the room, Dominika knew now that she had a tall request to make, and hoped with all of her body and soul that they'd accept.

"Mr. and Mrs. Crystal," the Russian girl asked with a desperate, yet hopeful look, "would you take me in as one of your own; I have no one now and I *really* want to honor my mother's dying wish, as well as avenge the death of my sister."

"I don't know, Dominika," Tori answered slowly. She started to say more, but Ted told her to sleep on it, plus he added he wanted a private word with Dominika. Tori nodded and gently kissed Dominika and left, leaving her husband alone with the orphaned Russian girl. Once they were alone, Dominika had to ask something that she'd been wondering about for quite a while that day.

"How come I don't have any pain or scars on me, Mr. Crystal," she asked, "I mean, shouldn't there be some kind of mark where Blohkin's bullet grazed my left calf?"

"All of us Crystals have 'hidden talents', Dominika," Ted explained, "and Kara is the healer of the family; that is why you don't have any scars on you." He went on to explain about how he was basically a psychic medium, a person able to communicate with the dead, Tori had sort of an eye for seeing the future, Kara was a psychic healer, Dinah had a super sonic kind of scream, nearly identical to her namesake, the Black Canary, and Barda was an empath, someone who picks up on emotional energy.

"However, Dominika, I believe there is more to you then you're letting on," he continued, "I have a sense that you have a hidden talent also."

"You and your family are truly amazing," Dominika answered with a slight blush, "but I do have a hidden talent; I'm a synesthete, which basically means I can read minds."

"How can you do it?"

"By how their face looks, and also through colors above their heads too."

"I had a hunch," Ted concluded, "plus, I've decided, here and now, to invite you to become part of our family."

"Really," Dominika cried happily. As soon as Ted nodded, she jumped into his arms, totally forgetting that she had nothing covering her body. Ted quietly reminded her, but also said not to fret too much since nobody was watching anyway. He then walked over to the dresser, and found a long shirt that he gave Dominika to cover herself. Once she'd gotten covered, Ted sat down next to her and explained they'd train her to be their fourth Warrior Princess. Dominika was a bit confused, but Ted told her it was a family thing and to give a more in depth telling later.

"Your training won't be easy," he explained further, "however, I'm confident you'll be able to do it, Dominika Crystal." Hearing that Ted was referring to her by his family's name made Dominika seem to swell with happiness.

"I like the sound of Crystal as my last name," Dominika sighed, "thank you Mr. Crystal, er I mean Father." She and Ted had a slight laugh but a good one.

"You're more than welcome, *Dushka*," Ted replied softly. He saw that Dominika was shocked, but told her that this was the only Russian word he knew how to translate to English.

"I'll tell you how I learned about State School Four, and that one word in the morning; right now, sleep, my daughter since you have a busy weekend ahead." Dominika nodded and moved herself under the blankets. Ted carefully and gently tucked his new daughter in and gently kissed her good night.

"Good night, Father," he heard Dominika call softly, "and thank you so much again." As Ted turned out the light and quietly left the room, Dominika sank peacefully into sleep.

CHAPTER 5

THE CRYSTALS AROSE SHORTLY AFTER sunrise the next day, except Dominika, since she wasn't used to getting up so early. After Ted and Tori finished getting ready for the day, they went over to the guestroom and carefully awoke their newest daughter. First, they asked her if she could describe Blohkin and his car, as well as her sister so that the local police would be able to, hopefully, find Marta's body. Next, Ted told Dominika about the **RED SPARROW** book trilogy by ex-CIA agent Jason Matthews, which was how he'd learned about State School Four. Finally, Ted stepped out of the room, since Dominika had to take off the shirt he'd given her to sleep in so that Tori could get her measurements in order to make her Warrior Princess outfit, as well as find out what her fashion sense was. Tori was surprised that Dominika's bust was a bit bigger than Barda's, considering that her body size was more in line with Dinah's. It was during this time that the Russian girl first noticed her adoptive mother's mismatched eyes, one was sky blue while the other was emerald green.

"Mother," Dominika asked, blushing slightly at what she'd just said, "why are your eyes two different colors?"

"They've been that way since I was born, Dominika," Tori replied, "I got made fun of a lot when I was your age because of them, but Ted was the first person, other than my parents, who thought my mismatched eyes were pretty, along with my bright red hair." Tori gave her very long, bright red hair a couple of quick whips.

"That sounds lovely, Mother," Dominika told Tori, surprised she felt herself sighing in the process.

You're lovely, Dominika Crystal," Tori said kindly. Then, Barda, Dinah, and Kara came into the room with some bundles in hand, telling their new sister that they were willing to give her some of their extra clothes, as well as shop for her. Dominika blushed heavily, but still graciously accepted everything. Once Tori and the triplets had all hugged her, they left Dominika alone so she could get ready for the day.

After showering and getting dressed in a halter top, which really showed off her bust, and shorts, she headed downstairs to join her new family for breakfast. When the family was halfway through their Mountain Man Breakfast, which Dominika found quite tasty, Ted called everyone's attention and stood.

"I have an announcement to make, y'all," he began, "I'd like for everyone to meet the newest member of the Crystal family: Dominika Crystal." The triplets were shocked, but quickly burst into cheers and applause at finding out that their friend was now their sister. This all caused Dominika to blush, since she'd never been so flattered in her entire life. Their father went on to explain the plan to train her as their fourth Warrior Princess and to bring Blohkin to justice for murdering Marta. Finally, he asked Dominika if she'd like to say anything and the Russian girl slowly rose to her feet.

"I'd like to thank all of you for taking me in for, this is going to sound very odd but, from the second I met all of you, I somehow felt like I belonged with you," she told everyone as a few joyful tears leaked out, "so again, thank you for helping me fulfill my birth mother's dream and I'm really looking forward to learning and training with you." Her new family applauded her as she returned to her seat. Once the table was cleared, Ted told Tori to have everyone to head over to the Workout House, their little at-home gym in one of the converted equipment sheds, and get training underway. Tori asked if he'd be joining them and Ted responded that he would, but after he made an important phone call. When the rest of the family had left the house, Ted got on the phone and called his old friend CJ Jones, who was the local sheriff. After two rings, the sheriff picked up.

"Covington police department, Sheriff Jones speaking," CJ answered.

"Hi, CJ, this Ted Crystal calling," Ted replied, "how have things been?"

"Hey man, it's been pretty quiet lately, but what's up?"

"I'll tell you that some other time, CJ, can you come out to the farm ASAP; I think there may be a Russian government assassin after my newest daughter."

"You didn't tell me Tori was having another, Ted," CJ exclaimed.

"She didn't, man, you know the two Borov sisters," Ted asked. CJ responded he did, and Ted told him why he had to get to the farm ASAP.

"You mean her sister was murdered, and then she escapes and ends up in the trunk of one of your family's Dodge Chargers looking like she went through a slasher flick," the sheriff gasped.

"Yes, and that guy is still on the loose," Ted finished.

"Say no more, I'm on my way; see you in fifteen minutes."

"That is a big ten-four; see you then." After hanging up with the sheriff, Ted hustled over to the Work out House, where training was going very well. He observed that Dominika had already worked up quite a sweat, but it didn't seem to be slowing her down any. In fact, it looked like she was moving just as swiftly and gracefully as Barda, Dinah, and Kara. Tori was pleased as well, seeing how well their adopted daughter was taking to her training like a fish to water.

When Tori signaled it was time for a cool down break, the girls headed for the fridge while Tori came over and talked to her husband.

"How is she doing, Honey," Ted asked his wife.

"She is doing so well it is unbelievable, Dear," Tori answered, "it's almost like she was born to be one of us."

"That's good to hear, my Love; I called CJ and he's coming over in a bit."

"What for?"

"We need to give him the information about Blohkin and Marta; that way the law can be on the look-out."

While their parents talked, Barda, Dinah, and Kara were enjoying conversation with their new sister.

"You seem to have a natural talent for what we're doing, Dominika," Dinah said, "I mean, you're mastering techniques in ten minutes that took us years to get right."

"Thank you, Dinah," Dominika giggled, blushing slightly. The Russian girl wasn't used to being the center of attention, and having people give her kind compliments, though she was certainly enjoying it.

"I have a feeling that when you complete your training, Sis, the men had better watch out," Barda proclaimed, "because they could end up getting hurt."

"Yes, but I'd know ahead of time to avoid them, Barda," Dominika remarked, "like all of you, I have a hidden talent." The Russian girl didn't expect her new sisters to lean closer, but they did. This seemed to make Dominika blush more heavily.

"What is your gift, Sis," all three asked.

"Hehe, I can read minds," Dominika answered with a small giggle. This made all three of her sisters exclaim, but with pride.

"Well, this for sure gives a whole new meaning to the term 'beauty and brains', ladies," Kara announced. Just then, their parents called, telling them it was time to resume their training. So, setting their beverages aside, the four princesses quickly got back to it, with Barda and Dinah working together on a review of techniques and Kara working with Dominika on speed and smoothness.

About fifteen minutes later, Ted and Tori announced that morning training was done, and it was time to head back to the house. On the way, they all noticed the sheriff pulling into the driveway. CJ got out of his patrol car and said his 'hi, how are you's' and then they all went inside. After a quick snack, the girls headed to the living room for a little rest and relaxation. When his daughters were out of the kitchen, Ted gave CJ all the information Dominika had given him about her sister and her sister's killer. CJ told him that he'd take everything down to the station and get the ball rolling. Ted also asked him if he could get the necessary papers so that the ball could get rolling on Dominika's defection and adoption. CJ replied that he'd see to that ASAP before leaving. Ted then called Dominika in to the kitchen and explained to her everything he'd told the sheriff, which made his adopted daughter begin to cry happy tears. The Russian girl was so overjoyed that she hugged her adoptive father hard and kissed both his cheeks.

"Thank you so much, Father," she cried happily, "I hope this process goes by fast."

"It will, *Dushka*," Ted told her, giving her a gentle one-arm hug, "I hope that soon your sister will get found and properly laid to rest." Dominika then raced back into the living room and told her sisters the news, which made them cheer and hug her. Still, Dominika was nervous about Blohkin and wasn't sure that when her trial came about, that she'd be able to get through it. However, she pushed all negative thoughts out of her mind and focused on the joy of the present.

CHAPTER 6

After Sheriff Jones collected the needed information, he quickly went back to the station and got everything rolling. Wanted posters were printed up and passed out, agencies were called, and paperwork was made ready. Within a span of only two hours, all of Covington and a few of the nearby towns knew about Blohkin and what had happened to Dominika's sister. Sadly, when the sheriff and a few deputies went to the little flat where Marta and Dominika had stayed, Marta's body was nowhere to be found. CJ told his deputies to keep looking around the property and then he drove over to Old Muscle Farm to deliver the news.

Ted, Tori, and their daughters were drag racing on their private strip when the sheriff arrived. He asked if he could speak to Ted and Dominika alone. So, Ted left Tori to get the next race, which was between Dinah and Kara, going while he and Dominika talked with CJ.

"A few deputies and I went to the flat, but we were unable to locate your sister's corpse", CJ told Dominika, with a touch of genuine sadness, "I sincerely apologize, Honey". For a moment, Dominika was at a total loss for words. Then, as the words sank further in, she let out a near blood curdling scream and collapsed to her knees, crying.

"No, Marta", she sobbed, "you don't deserve that, sister"! Ted and CJ tried to calm her down, but she shook them off and ran into the barn. The sheriff turned back to Ted.

"I'm sorry, man", he said, "I wish I could've delivered good news".

"Its OK, CJ", Ted told him, "I think, no I KNOW how to get my new daughter smiling again".

"How", the sheriff asked.

"Trust me", Ted replied, "I got this". He then told CJ to go back to town and tell the funeral home to get prepped for a funeral. The sheriff was a bit confused, but agreed and headed off. Once the sheriff had left, Ted then went to the barn to find Dominika. He eventually found her, still crying, over by his 'top secret' car. Ted slowly made his way over and gently touched Dominika's shoulder. She turned to her adopted father, her bright sapphire/aquamarine eyes still brimming with tears, and hugged him.

"Oh Father", she sniffed, "I'll never be able to tell my sister goodbye now".

"What do you mean, Honey", Ted asked, though he had a slight hunch as to what his adopted daughter was about to say.

"Blohkin and his pigs took her back to Russia to be buried as a traitor", Dominika cried, "she wasn't a traitor in any way". She then began crying again, with Ted gently comforting her. However, after a little bit, she calmed down enough for Ted to tell her something.

"You *are* going to be able to tell your sister goodbye, Dominika", he told her, adding, "and she won't be going back to Russia". Dominika looked at her adopted father in complete confusion.

"How is that possible, Father", she asked, "you can't turn back time".

"Actually, *Dushka*, I can", Ted replied as he whipped off the tarp. Once again, Bunny, Ted's 1981 DeLorean DMC-12 which had been modified for time travel, was revealed. Dominika was a bit skeptical at first, but her mind reading ability told her to believe her adopted father. Ted then asked her for the time that she and Blohkin had left the flat the day that Marta had been murdered and she'd come into their family. As they both climbed into Bunny, Ted typed the information into the time circuits and they soon were off.

After accelerating to 88 miles per hour, Dominika was surprised when they actually came to a stop near the flat on that day. Though when she looked at the time circuits, she noticed that the time was different then what she'd told her adopted father.

"I brought us here five minutes after you and Blohkin left here", Ted told her, "that way, we'd run the least risk of being seen by you or him". At that, they quickly parked Bunny and hurried into the flat. Of course, they found Marta's body lying near the door, as well as the knife that Blohkin had used to slit her throat. Ted quickly put on gloves and found a plastic bag in the kitchen to stash the knife so they could give it to the sheriff when they got back. Then, he and Dominika carefully wrapped Marta in a sheet and quickly got her back outside and placed her in Bunny's trunk. Dominika was getting back in the DeLorean when she saw Ted quickly digging through the trash.

"Father, what are you doing", she asked.

"Getting fuel for the time circuits and the flux capacitor", he replied. After throwing the items he'd collected into a small fusion generator on the back of the car, Ted quickly got the destination time entered into the time circuits and they were back in the current time before they knew it.

Once they were back in the current time, Ted drove himself and Dominika over to the funeral home, where the director was waiting. After the funeral home people had taken Marta's body inside, Ted quickly called the sheriff and asked if he and a few deputies could come over to the funeral home. He also called home and told Tori to get Barda, Dinah, and Kara into some formal clothes for Marta's small funeral. When he'd hung up the phone, Ted heard Marta's voice.

"Thank you, Mr. Crystal", she told him, "I'm sad I can't be a part of your family, but I trust you to take care of my sister".

"You're more than welcome, Marta", Ted replied quietly, "we will". Soon CJ and two deputies arrived and Ted gave them the knife for processing. Shortly afterward, the rest of his family arrived for the funeral. It was a short service, but a bitter sweet one. When Marta's casket was lowered into the grave at the local cemetery, Dominika gave her sister a small farewell. When the Crystals got back home that evening, Dominika thanked her adopted family for helping her lay her sister to rest in peace.

After a light dinner, Barda, Dinah, Kara, and Dominika headed for bed. However, they all gathered in Dominika's room and expressed their feelings, which gave Dominika a good deal of comfort. The Crystals then bid each other good night and went to their separate rooms. Little did any of them know that their newest family member would end up seeing a slight glimpse of her Warrior Princess trial, and her adopted mother would see a deadly scary battle, that very night.

CHAPTER 7

As Tori settled into bed next to her husband, she couldn't help but feel nervous about them taking her in. However, Ted assured her that it was almost like when he'd taken her in. This seemed to calm Tori, but for some reason she was still feeling nervous.

"I think my ability is kicking in, Honey," she said.

"What are you seeing, Tori," Ted asked his wife.

"I think it may be a showing of her trial."

"Maybe sleeping on it will make things clearer." Tori seemed to agree with her husband and soon she and Ted were fast asleep. However, Tori was right about her ability to see the future showing her a glimpse of their adopted daughter's upcoming trial. In the vision, she saw herself, Ted, as well as Barda, Dinah, and Kara all fighting against Blohkin and his fellow government agents. She saw that they were able to take them by surprise at the beginning with their two tanks and their off road cars, but then the tide turned and she, Ted, and their biological daughters were all out of the fight and Dominika ended up captured. Also, Dominika's mind reading ability was picking up on everything, and soon Tori and Ted were awakened by their adopted daughter screaming from across the hall. They raced over to her room, but it seemed that the triplets had heard her sooner, for they were already in the room, trying to help her calm down.

"Dominika, are you alright," Tori asked.

"I am now," Dominika whispered, "it seems I was picking up on something you were thinking about, Mother." Her sisters looked from Dominika to Tori with surprise, but Tori didn't reveal anything, except to Dominika who was reading her thoughts.

"What is going on, Mom," Kara asked.

"I saw a vision of our newest princess's trial, girls," Tori answered, "however, I'm not ready to share the details with all of you just yet." Dinah, Barda, and Kara knew that their mother wasn't joking, so they each kissed Dominika and their mother good night and left the room. Tori, however, remained in the room with Dominika. Sitting down on her adopted daughter's bed, she hugged her before asking how Dominika knew that she'd seen a vision of her upcoming trial.

"I can read minds, Mother," Dominika replied, "I've been able to read minds from the time I was very young; it has helped Marta and I through some tough times."

"That is amazing, Honey," Tori responded, adding, "I guess it doesn't really sleep does it?"

"I guess not," Dominika said with a little giggle.

"Well, I suppose I should tell you what I was seeing," Tori said with a heavy sigh. So, she explained what she'd seen in her vision. Dominika was frightened by what her adopted mother told her, but she felt that it was something she had to go through if she wanted to avenge her birth sister's death and fulfill her birth mother's dying wish.

"It sounds like I have no choice but to face this, Mother," Dominika said with a heavy sigh.

"You're right, Sweetheart, but Ted, myself, and your new sisters will be beside you every step of the way."

"Thank you, Mother." At that Tori bid Dominika good night and the whole family went to sleep.

The next morning, Dominika came down into the kitchen and decided to make some Russian pancakes and some eggs for her new family. The Russian pancakes were lighter and airier then regular pancakes and had Dominika added a little chopped bacon into them for some added flavor. The eggs she did scrambled and had just finished setting the table when her adopted family came in.

"I wanted to make breakfast to show my gratitude to you," she explained. Everyone thanked her and helped her get everything on the table. Soon, they were all enjoying Dominika's offerings, and when they expressed it, she blushed and giggled, but thanked them. As they were finishing, Tori told Dominika that the triplets had some more of their lightly used clothes for her in her room, as well as some new items that the triplets had purchased. Dinah leaned over and whispered that it was mostly leather things that they didn't like or want anymore, but that were still in excellent shape and some new leather items that would look great on their new sister.

"We want our new sister to look as hot and gorgeous as possible," Kara added softly.

"Thank you," Dominika whispered back. After the family had finished and the kitchen was cleaned up, Dominika hurried back up to her room to get ready. When she arrived, she saw all the clothes that her sisters had given her and she was excited, especially by the leather, since she and Marta had loved leather clothes. When she heard her sisters come up the stairs, she ran out of her room and hugged them.

"Thank you sisters," Dominika cried happily, "thank you so much."

"Ahh, you're welcome, sister," the triplets said together, blushing and then laughing. They all then headed into their own rooms to get dressed for church. Now, the Crystals weren't really into dressing formally, unless absolutely necessary. So, Tori was wearing a beige skater dress and black leather ankle boots with three inch heels and

Ted wore a simple shirt and shorts, even though it was October. Then, the triplets came downstairs, each wearing a reasonable top and a leather skirt of some kind, all in black, along with leather over the knee boots with four inch heels. Finally Dominika came down last and she was wearing a sky blue halter top, a black leather pencil skirt, and calf high leather boots with four inch heels.

"Do I look appropriate," she asked.

"In our book, you sure do," Kara answered. The family then headed out to where Ted had pulled up Fast Feline, a red 2016 Dodge Charger Hellcat. Once everyone was buckled in, they headed off for the church.

It only took a little while to get to the church, and Dominika thought it was a wonderful little country church. The mass was lovely and Dominika loved the readings about how the people of the Bible were always being told, by the prophets, the angels, and by Jesus, to not be afraid. *I know I must go through with my trial to avenge my birth sister's death and to fulfill my birth mother's dying wish,* she thought, *and I feel that with my adopted family's help, I will be able to do it.* After mass, Ted drove them over to the family business, Crystal Classics and Customs, to show Dominika what they did for a living. As they led her around the facility, Dominika was truly amazed by the kinds of cars that were in the shop, and even more amazed when her new sisters told her that they sometimes had to leave school early to come and help out.

"Do you worry about not being able to finish your school work," Dominika asked.

"Not at all," Dinah replied.

"Yeah, Mom and Dad told the school officials before our freshman year that we'd sometimes be called to the shop to help out with the workload," Barda added, "even though the staff here is awesome."

Dominka was shown all the areas of the shop, even the area where cars were customized to what the customer wanted. The triplets said that the customization area was their favorite to help out in, and it was their parents' favorite part of the business also.

"When a client brings in a car, and they tell us that they've always wanted to turn it into something awesome and unique but can't figure out what they'd like it to be," Tori explained, "that is when we *really* get excited."

"Yeah," Kara added, "we sit down with them and talk over what kinds of things they really like, such as monsters or superheroes, and then we draw up a few ideas and they draw up a few ideas and we look over everything and that is how the client and us usually come up with a custom design for the vehicle."

"So, you and the client talk about what *both* parties think would be cool and then you design it with them," Dominika asked.

"Exactly, Dominika," Ted told her, "for we feel that if you want your car customized but you're a bit stuck on where to go, the customizer and the client should try to come with a design together, so that way it is clear for the customizer, and the client will know that they're going to be getting an awesome and unique vehicle at the end of the process." Glancing up at a clock, it was almost eleven, so the family decided to head home for lunch.

When they got back to Old Muscle Farm and had gotten Fast Feline stashed back in his stall, Tori and Ted suggested that the triplets give Dominika a good look around the garage and the little aircraft hangar. Once their parents had left, the triplets showed Dominika around the barn, pointing out some of their favorite cars, such as the General Lee, Black Beauty, and Ecto-1. They even showed their adopted sister Ecto-1's interior, which they used as a base camp whenever the family went out on paranormal investigation trips. In addition, they showed Dominika some of the evidence of the paranormal that they'd collected from a few of their investigations, including some EVPs (Electronic Voice Phenomena) and photos. After showing off a few of their exotic cars, a few of the Ferraris, Lamborghinis, and Bugattis, they headed over to the aircraft hangar and their sister was amazed to see a surplus B-17 bomber and a surplus P-47 fighter. The Fokker DR-1 triplane replica was nice also, but what really took Dominika by surprise was the replica of the first XF-11 spy plane designed and built by billionaire Howard Hughes. Her sisters told her that theirs was the same thing, but the cameras were all there, still cameras for color and black-and-white photos as well as black-and-white and color video cameras, plus a night vision camera in the nose and the rear of the left boom. When they were leaving the hangar, they saw their mother calling that lunch was ready.

As they dined on some homemade tacos and salsa, Tori told them that she'd had a vision. In it, Blohkin and his goons from the Russian government would try to ambush the girls on their way home from school this upcoming week.

"What should we do," Dominika asked.

"The only thing we can do, sister," Barda replied, "out drive and outsmart those rotten Ruskies." This made everyone laugh, even Dominika.

"So, basically, we're going to make Blohkin and his men look like *idiotikas*," she asked.

"You got it, sister," Dinah answered. Everyone laughed about this, and continued enjoying lunch. After dessert, the girls went out to the barn. As they were heading over, they told Dominika that the General needed a bath. Dominika said she'd be pleased to help out and so once Dinah had gotten the Charger moved outside, and the soap had been mixed and the other cleaning supplies had been brought out, they got done to business. Barda shined up the wheels and tires, Kara cleaned the windows, and Dinah and Dominika polished up the body, with Dinah starting in the back and Dominika starting at the front. Once the General was all shined up, the girls started having fun with the soap and the hose until they were all dripping wet and giggling hysterically, even Dominika.

"That was fun," Dominika said breathlessly.

"Yeah, but we'd better try to dry off and get the General back in the barn," Dinah replied. Realizing that there was no way any of them would get dry fast enough, the girls threw a dry towel inside the Charger and Dinah carefully got him back in his stall. When they got back inside the house, Tori and Ted noticed them as they headed upstairs. However, they both just looked at each other and laughed.

After the girls had changed into some dry clothes, they all went downstairs to the game room in the basement. Dominika enjoyed learning how to play pool and she was able to beat her adopted sisters at darts. Plus, she really loved the old entertainment center that was full of board games, except for X-wing miniatures, the Star Wars game that had you take miniature models of actual Star Wars ships and battle with them, since there were too many pieces to store in one container. Dominika watched Barda and Kara play a round of X-wing and thought it would be fun to learn, but after her trial.

Soon, Ted called the girls upstairs for dinner. As the family enjoyed their salmon fillets and shrimp with cocktail sauce, Tori told them all that she'd seen that Blohkin and his goons were going to still try and catch Dominika as the girls were making their way home from school during the upcoming week.

"We have ideas on how we can outdrive him, Mom," Barda told Tori.

"I'm sure you girls do," Tori replied, "still be careful."

"We will," Dinah said confidently. Once their dessert of homemade lava cake was finished, they all cleared the table and cleaned everything. Before the girls went to bed, they all gathered in the library on the second floor. Dominika was a little confused, but she went in with her adopted sisters.

"What exactly are we doing," she asked.

"We do this every Sunday before we go to sleep, sis," Dinah explained, "we simply sit in a circle, hold hands, and focus our energy."

"Like a form of meditation?"

"Something like that, though we draw strength from each other for the week ahead." As Dominika joined Barda, Kara, and Dinah in their circle, she felt like she belonged there. She closed her eyes, like her adopted sisters and focused her energy. As she did this, she could feel her energy combining with her sisters' energy. After a little bit of time, they opened their eyes, hugged each other, and headed off to bed, for they all seemed to know that this upcoming week was going to test them all like never before.

CHAPTER 8

On Monday morning, the Crystals were all down in the kitchen, except for Dominika. Of course Ted and Tori had asked the triplets where their sister was, and all that Barda, Dinah, and Kara said was that she was getting ready. It was about five minutes later that Dominika finally came into the kitchen, and did she look incredible. Their adopted sister wore a black tank top with a hot rod on it, a semi tight black leather skirt, and white sneakers. Plus, she'd added a little curl to her rich brown hair. Her adopted family also saw she wore pale red lip gloss and black eye liner.

"How do I look," she asked slightly nervous but still confident. It took a minute, but her family soon let out cheers and told her she looked awesome. Once that situation was taken care of, they all sat down for breakfast. Dominika told her family that all the clothes they'd given her, whether handed down or bought, she loved, especially the leather. When asked why, she gave an amazing answer, and it jogged the triplet's memory of something she and Marta had told them once.

"My birth mother was an actress and a singer," she explained, "so when Marta and I were little, we'd sometimes get into her fancy clothes and try to act and perform like her." She did blush slightly, but everyone just gave an understanding little chuckle. When asked if she had any songs her mother sang, Dominika said she had them in her room and that they could listen after school.

"Well, speaking of school," Ted announced, "it's about time for you girls to start heading there; Dominika since you actually do have a license why don't you pick a car and take it?" He'd come across Dominika's driver's license when he and the family had helped Dominika the day she'd come into their family injured.

"You mean it, Father," she gasped, her eyes starting to overflow with happy tears.

"Certainly, there's plenty to pick from." Dominika let out an excited squeal and followed her sisters out to the barn. As Barda, Kara, and Dinah got their own cars ready, Dominika looked around, trying to decide which one would be her ride. She finally settled on Black Sparrow, a 1973 Nissan Skyline GT-R. Once her ride was selected, Dominika followed her sisters and their American Muscle Cars out of the barn and off to the school.

Ten minutes later, the Crystals arrived at the high school and parked together. Once all four had exited their cars, they all noticed that all the other students were watching them, especially Dominika. Now, the Russian girl did start to get a little worried, but her sisters just whispered to her to act natural, which she did. Surprisingly, she felt more at ease, not just from being with her adopted sisters, but because of what she'd driven up in, and in what she was wearing. *Amazing,* she thought, *I'm gaining confidence in myself, which I know for sure I'll need.* In fact, the whole day felt awesome to her. People were saying "hi" to her and giving her kind smiles and thumbs up. The morning flew by fairly fast. At lunch, the Crystals sat at their usual table and began their chatter, though the conversation flowed over to their new sister's trial and whether or not Blohkin would try to make an appearance.

"I feel that he will, sisters," Dominika said quietly, "I'm very sure of it."

"Well, in that case we'd better keep our wits about us," Barda declared, "as well as keep our ears on and eyes peeled."

"One problem, I find, is how are we going to know what his cronies look like," Kara piped up.

"I know the names," Dominika answered.

"How do you know that, Dominika," Dinah asked.

"Marta and I saw his contacts list on a table once; when we get back home, I'll have Father tell the sheriff." Just then, the bell rang, and everyone was off to the afternoon classes. Dominika's confidence kept building, particularly in art class when a classmate asked her if he was interpreting a painting right. He thanked her for her input, which did make her blush, but she felt happy instead of embarrassed.

Once school let out for the day, the Crystals headed out to get their cars and head for home. However, Kara quickly moved beside Dominika and whispered to her that she saw Blohkin's Lincoln pull up at the front of the school. Dominika got nervous, but she was surprised when the nervousness left her as quickly as it had come. *They are protecting me, but soon I'll have to protect them*, she thought, *however, I feel now that I'm up for the challenge of my trial, whenever it comes; Lord, I hope I'll be able to pass through it and earn my Warrior Princess title.* Thankfully, Blohkin didn't see her, and she and her sisters got to their cars and headed back to Old Muscle Farm. When the sisters got home, they told their parents that they'd seen Blohkin's Lincoln at the school, but that he hadn't seen Dominika. Ted and Tori were shocked, but relieved at the same time. Also, Dominika added that when Kara had told her she'd seen Blohkin, she'd gotten nervous but the feeling had left as soon as it had come.

"That's a good thing, Dominika," Ted told her, "you're getting more confident in yourself and that desire to fight for your freedom is still burning bright and strong."

"I understand that, Father," Dominika replied, "though I'm sure I'll still be nervous until after my trial is over, considering what it may entail, according to what Mother saw." Everyone seemed to pause when their newest family member said this, remembering how her mind reading ability had picked up on Tori's future seeing.

"That is understandable, Sis," Barda piped up, "but we have to prepare ourselves, all of us."

"Barda's right, Dominika," Dinah added, "it won't just be a trial for you, it'll be a trial for all of us."

"They're right, Sweetheart," Tori announced, "when the triplets had their trials, everyone was involved in some way, so it won't be anything new for us."

"Besides, we're a family and we don't fight alone," Kara finished, "we stand together and fight together." With that, the Crystals all came together for a group hug. The girls headed to the living room for homework while their parents stayed in the kitchen to make the chicken and rice for dinner. Once it was ready, Ted called the girls in as Tori set the table. Over the course of dinner, the usual questions got asked, like how the school day had gone, but after a few minutes Dominika was asked how she felt she was doing. Their adopted daughter was a bit caught off guard, but she quickly got past her surprise and spoke up.

"I'm feeling a lot more confident in myself, mainly due to having a sense of inclusion and belonging," she replied, adding, "not to mention wearing leather as much as the rest of you makes me even more confident." She went on to tell them that when she and Marta would put their mother's leather clothes and things on, it made them feel invincible. She ended up giggling, which made her blush as well. What really amazed Dominika is that when she tried to apologize for it, her sisters told her that all of them had that odd habit, having inherited it from their mom. Dominika looked at Tori who confirmed that it was indeed true that she giggled when she blushed.

"I'm in shock," Dominika responded, "it seems I truly was meant to be part of your family."

"Indeed it does, Dominika," Ted said, "speaking of which, something lovely just came in the mail."

"What is it, Dad," the triplets asked. Ted pushed back his chair and rose to his feet. Kara whispered to Dominika that when their dad did this, it meant he had something important to say. Dominika nodded and straightened in her chair.

"Everyone, this is amazing news indeed," Ted announced, "for today, we are now, officially and legally, a family of six; Dominika Crystal, you're legally and officially one of us now." The triplets immediately started cheering and clapping and Dominika burst into tears of joy. Everyone gathered around her and hugged her.

"Thank you, thank you," Dominika sobbed happily. After the announcement, the table was cleared and before everyone headed off to bed, Ted and Tori explained that Saturday's training would be on their obstacle course, one with driving and the other was a physical fitness one. Dominika got excited, but little did she know that a small part of her trial was to take place on the physical fitness obstacle course.

CHAPTER 9

Saturday dawned, and Dominika arose along with the rest of her family. Since the rest of the week had gone smoothly, and quickly, she was feeling good but knew that eventually Blohkin and his goons were going to come looking for her; it was all a matter of how soon that would happen. However, she tried to think positive thoughts and focus on the present. When she got downstairs to the kitchen, she was surprised to see Barda already there and dressed, finishing off a can of NOS energy drink.

"Good morning, Barda," Dominika said, "I didn't think I'd see you up so early."

"Yeah well I had dawn patrol today, so I didn't really have a choice," Barda replied.

"Dawn patrol?"

"Yeah, every morning one of us patrols around the outer ring of our property; Mom and Dad usually do it during the week, since we have school, but one of us gets to do it on the weekend." Barda explained that they had five vehicles in the barn from the **FAST AND FURIOUS** franchise that were modified for off-roading: a 1970 Dodge Charger, a twenty first century Dodge Challenger, a 1968 Chevrolet Camaro Z28, a vehicle called a Rallye Fighter, and a Peterbilt tow truck.

"Wow, that sounds interesting, Sister," Dominika gasped in awe, "which did you use?"

"I used the Camaro, since I love GM products." Just then, Kara and Dinah came into the kitchen for breakfast. They told Barda and Dominika that practice on the obstacle course would start a little after nine that morning. Once that was announced, the sisters all got to work on breakfast. Barda helped, but she'd already eaten awhile ago so when they all sat down, she just had some pieces of bacon while her sisters had a full Mountain Man breakfast. As they were finishing, their parents entered the kitchen.

"Well, it's lovely to see our darling princesses having a meal together," Ted said, which made all of them blush, "hopefully y'all can get ready quickly so our training can start; though keep your eyes peeled, girls, I thought I saw an ominous looking vehicle go up and down the road lately this week." This announcement seemed to put everyone on edge, but especially Dominika. *Oh God*, she thought, *Blohkin and his goons have tracked me here*. However, she pushed her fear aside with an iron force from deep within her soul. Tori then told everyone who'd start on which course. Kara and Dinah would start off on the dirt trail course with Dirt Devil, their off road Charger, and Dirt Challenge, the off road Challenger while Barda and Dominika would begin on the physical fitness course. Once they'd gotten around the course twice, they'd switch.

After clearing the table, the girls headed to their rooms to get ready. Once they'd changed into sports bras, leather leggings, and sneakers, the sisters met at the top of the stairs to wish each other good luck. Just before they headed down, Dominika promised she'd share her mother's music and photos with everyone later on, which was met with much happy anticipation. Once downstairs and out by the barn, Kara and Dinah drove Barda and Dominika over to the physical fitness course in Dirt Devil and Dirt Challenge. When their sisters were dropped off, Kara and Dinah took off down the dirt track course, while Barda and Dominika started off on their physical fitness course.

Meanwhile, Blohkin and a couple of his friends had indeed tracked Dominika to Old Muscle Farm. However they hadn't quite figured out how to get at her without her adopted family noticing. So when they drove past and saw her and Barda heading off on the obstacle course, they pulled onto a dirt path that went along the side of the Crystals' property.

"If we can slip in and snatch her, boys," Blohkin told his fellow goons, "we'll be in the clear." With that, they began to charge toward her and Barda.

Unfortunately, Dominika and Barda had caught sight of Blohkin's car coming up the path, and headed for the part of the course that required them to go up into and through the trees. *Oh no*, Dominika thought, *he's found me; God help me!* As she and Barda got up into the trees, Barda fired a small signal flare, which both girls had been given in case an emergency happened. Over on the dirt track course, Dinah spotted Barda's flare and alerted Kara that something was wrong. Without wasting a minute, they headed for the physical fitness course.

Just when Blohkin and his friends thought they had Dominika right where they wanted her, Dinah and Kara appeared on the scene. Kara rammed the rear of Blohkin's Lincoln with Dirt Challenge's front, which made it spin and caused the right side tires on Dirt Devil to run right over the hood, bending and crumpling it in the process. Dominika jumped into Dirt Devil through the top hatch while Barda jumped on top of Dirt Challenge and climbed in through the window. Once their sisters were safe, all four of them raced ahead and vanished into the woods.

As Blohkin brought his Lincoln to a stop, he and his goons were cussing out loud in Russian that they'd missed their prey just when it seemed to be in their hands. Now, they realized, the police were going to be alerted and that stake outs would be put in place, so they figured they'd better clear out as quick as possible. And they did clear out, only it was a bit slower since Blohkin's car had been damaged, but they cleared out. *Dominika Borov*, Blohkin swore to himself, *I'm going to catch you and send you immediately to Sparrow School if it's the last thing I do*. Little did he or any of his fellow goons know that was going to be way easier said then done.

CHAPTER 10

As the Crystals raced through the woods, they all realized that they were shaking with nerves, Dominika the most. *Heaven help me*, she prayed, *I don't want to be a Sparrow; even worse, I don't want to end up like my birth sister Marta.* As she was thinking this, her sapphire/aquamarine eyes started to leak out tears and she began to softly sob. Dinah heard her sister starting to cry and made a CB call to Kara, telling her and Barda to pull over and they needed to regroup. As the girls climbed out of their off road cars, Dominika all of a sudden let out an anguished wail and collapsed to her knees, with rivers of tears running down her beautiful face.

"I can't do it, I just can't," she sobbed, "I'll never be able to shake Blohkin and his goons for as long as I live; I'll never be free." Just then, she felt three pairs of strong, yet warm, arms wrap around her. She slowly lifted her head and saw her new sisters had circled her and were hugging her.

"Calm down, sis," Barda said soothingly, "we've all been scared in our lives; just because we're Warrior Princesses doesn't mean we aren't allowed to get scared."

"R-really," Dominika asked, sniffling.

"Certainly, Dominika," Dinah replied, "before we had our own trials, we all were pretty much scared stiff; I know mine was probably the most horrifying."

"It was," Dominika asked.

"Yes, it was," Kara announced, "poor Dinah was nearly naked, very cut up, and was just about to get turned into shark bait when we finally rescued her; however, her trial had long passed by then."

"What were your trials like, sisters," Dominika wanted to know.

"I think that should be a conversation after your trial is done, sis," Dinah decided.

"Agreed," Barda chimed in, "though I will say, Dominika, you were really nailing it on the obstacle course before those rotten ruskies showed up." When she heard Blohkin and his gang referred to as rotten ruskies, Dominika cracked up, which surprised her sisters.

"Sisters," Dominika giggled, "that is the only way to refer to Russians like him, though I call the leader 'Mr. Pinhead' since he only cares about himself; I'll wager that if his brain were dynamite, he couldn't light a candle." They all started laughing at that, though Kara reminded everyone it was "if brains were dynamite you couldn't blow your nose". However, that made their adopted sister laugh even harder.

Barda then happened to glance at her watch and realized they needed to get home for lunch. As the sisters reached the main barnyard area, they saw their parents standing in the driveway next to a large crate. Bringing their cars to a halt, the girls all jumped down and told Ted and Tori what had happened.

"We're well aware of it," Ted replied, "your mother and I were listening in on the CB." He went on to explain that he'd already called the sheriff, but were intrigued when their father told them that he'd asked CJ to not do a full on stake out, for he had a hunch that is what Blohkin and his goons were expecting them to do. Instead, the local police were just going to do drive-by patrols. However, the girls were curious about what was in the large crate.

"This is a late birthday present for your mom," Ted explained, "Tori, I know you're not expecting this at all, but go ahead and reveal what it is." With that, he handed Tori a crow bar and stood back as he and his daughters watched her pry open one end of the crate. When Tori looked inside, she let out a loud, excited squeal of surprise and shock.

"What is it, Mom," the girls all asked at the same time.

"It's the 1966 Ford GT40 MkII driven by Ken Miles and Dennis Helume at the 1966 24 Hours of Le Mans." At this, their daughters all ran over to look inside the crate. Sure enough, there sat Ford number 1, chassis number 1015, from the 1966 Le Mans race.

"Thank you so much, Ted," Tori cried happily, hugging her husband.

"Aww, you're welcome, Darlin'," Ted replied, giving her a kiss on the cheek, "let's get him out of that crate and into his new stall."

After completely breaking down the crate, the Crystals finally got the newest member of their automotive family, who they'd named Kenny in honor of Ken Miles, into his new stall in the barn. Then, the family headed back to the house. Ted and Tori headed for the kitchen to make lunch while their daughters headed upstairs to rest and change their clothes. When Dominika got to her room, she found her backpack and dug through it until she finally found her mother's photos and CDs, as well as all of her mother's sexy leather concert outfits. She was a bit worried about them, since her backpack had gotten wet when she'd been thrown into the pond when her bike tire hit the rock, but she'd put them inside a small metal box, which protected all of the photos and CDs from harm and the clothes had been near the outer part of her backpack, so they were dry and good. *Thank God*, she thought, *these are all I have left of my birth mother, and I'd have been really crushed if these were ruined.* After collecting everything, she headed down to basement recreation room with her sisters for some rest and relaxation.

Once the girls had gotten settled, Dinah asked Dominika if she'd found her mother's photos and CDs.

"I have, sisters," Dominika announced, revealing the cases, "here they are, thankfully unhurt from when I fell in the pond." They all had a small giggle then asked their new sister to pop one into the player. Once Dominika had the CD in, she told the others she and Marta had often danced to their mother's songs and told them she'd perform for them, if they wished.

"Let's see how you are, sis," Barda said, clapping, "go for it."

"Hehe, as you wish, Barda," Dominika giggled. She quickly struck a pose, then the music began. Barda, Dinah, and Kara watched in awe and amazement at their new sister dancing effortlessly to her birth mother's voice. The Crystals watched their adopted sister dance through every song on the CD and when the CD was done, they all stood up, cheering and clapping. Dominika had broken a sweat, but was overjoyed to see her family clapping and cheering for her. Plus, she saw the wispy forms of her birth mother and birth sister clapping and cheering also.

"Wow, Dominika," Kara exclaimed, "your dancing is amazing."

"Totally," Dinah agreed, "I've never seen anyone dance that effortlessly in my life."

"Thank you so much, sisters," Dominika replied, blushing heavily, which made her giggle even more, even though she was tired from dancing. Then, they all settled down for a movie. Dinah ended up picking **FORD VS. FERRARI** and they all got together on the couch.

When it got to the telling of the 1966 Le Mans, and Dominika saw the GT40 on the screen, she asked quietly if the car they'd just received was the one on-screen. Kara replied that the car on-screen was a replica and the one they'd gotten was the actual Ford GT40 Mark II that Ken Miles had driven at the actual 1966 Le Mans race. As the race continued, it was amazing to Dominika how different it was in 1966 then it was in modern times. She'd heard about the 24 hour race at Le Mans, but had never really grasped what it took to actually get through it. After the movie, Barda asked Dominika if she could have her mother's CDs. Dominika was a bit reluctant, but Barda promised that she'd give them back in a couple of hours. Dominika agreed then, and Barda set off for her room. When Dominika asked Dinah and Kara what Barda was up to, they told her that Barda was working on something for Dominika, but wouldn't say what it was.

After about an hour and a half, Barda knocked on Dominika's bedroom door. Dominika let her sister in, and Barda handed her back the CDs along with a little item wrapped in colored paper.

"What's this, Barda," Dominika asked.

"A little something from your new sisters to you, Dominika," Barda answered. Dominika unwrapped the item and saw that it was an iPod, with her mother's music on it. When Barda saw the shocked look on her sister's face, she offered an explanation.

"We all have iPods with our family music on them, Sis," she told Dominika, "our family *loves* Taylor Swift, but we all have other songs on our own individual pods; and I figured you'd like your birth mother's music on yours, along with Taylor Swift's songs and a little something extra." Barda showed Dominika that she'd put the song **ROAR** by Katy Perry on hers. She went on to say that she'd gone and added this song to all the iPods, since it was so inspiring and empowering.

"Kara, Dinah, and myself have sort of adopted this song as our kind of 'power-up anthem', since it makes you feel like you can do what you dream of."

"Thank you, Barda," Dominika replied, a few happy tears sliding out of her sapphire/aquamarine eyes.

"Ahh, you're welcome, Dominika," Barda told her, giving Dominika a hug. Barda then left Dominika to her own devices, and so she thought she'd listen to some of the other songs on the iPod, as well as the music videos. Dominika absolutely loved listening to her birth mother's songs on the pod, and was even more surprised when she saw the music videos of her birth mother' s songs that Barda had managed to locate. Finally, she decided to watch the music video for **ROAR**. The Russian girl was amazed at how Katy had changed from frightened cast away to jungle queen. Plus, she realized that Barda was right. It was a 'power-up anthem', for she suddenly felt her birth family there with her telling her that her new family were going to be alright, as well as Dominika herself. *This is just what I needed*, she thought, *if I keep up my training, and keep my confidence in myself high, I'll get through my trial.* Just then Kara knocked on Dominika's door to tell her dinner was ready.

"I'll be right down," Dominika called. A few minutes later, the Crystals were settling in for a lovely dinner of meatloaf, potatoes, and some assorted veggies. Dominika thought everything was delicious, and was thoroughly enjoying the evening chatter. When they were through the main course, Ted rose to his feet.

"Everyone, I have a feeling you're probably wondering why our family has acquired the Ford GT40 that Ken Miles drove at the 1966 Le Mans," he began, "well, I'll tell: it's not just because I love that car but because we're entered in a 24 hour race at Thanksgiving this year, and the two members of our family who will drive..." Everyone at the table held their breath, for they weren't sure who'd be chosen. Finally, after a full two minutes, Ted said the names.

"Dominika and Kara," he proclaimed. Everyone cheered, except Dominika for she was sitting at her place in shock. However, it was more joy shock then horror shock, and she soon snapped out of it and started sobbing tears of joy as her family surrounded her and

Kara and gave them both big hugs. Plus, she saw her birth family in the background, cheering for her also.

"Thank you, everyone," she cried happily through her tears, "thank you so much." With that, everyone got up and helped clear the table and then had a quick dessert. Once everyone had finished, the girls started heading upstairs for their rooms, but Ted and Tori asked Dominika if she'd stay back for a minute.

"What is it," she asked, already nervous.

"Well, Tori had another vision, Dominika," Ted informed her, "and your trial is drawing nearer, Dushka."

"Did it tell exactly when my trial will occur?"

"Unfortunately no, Dominika," Tori told her adopted daughter, "but this happened when the triplets had their trials also."

"So, just keep your ears on and eyes peeled, Honey."

"I will, Father."

"Alright, best head up with your sisters, y'all have school tomorrow." With that, Dominika headed upstairs to her room. After she'd finished brushing her hair, she noticed that there was a CD player in her room that she hadn't seen there before. However, she did remember that as she'd been heading to the stairs to come down for dinner, she saw Dinah go into her room, but hadn't asked why. Now she knew: Dinah put the CD player in her room as a gift. Going over to it, she saw the little note that told her to use it to enjoy the music of her old family and her new family. It concluded with the phrase, "With kindness, your loving sisters Barda, Dinah, and Kara". So, before she went to bed, Dominika went to all three of her sisters' rooms and thanked them one by one. They finally all gathered at the door to Dominika's room and fell into a group hug.

"Thank you again, sisters," Dominika told them.

"You're welcome, Dominika," her sisters replied all at once, which made them all blush and laugh, even Dominika. After one more group hug, they all went to their separate rooms and turned in for the night. Again, little did any of them know that over the course of that whole week, they'd have shake Blohkin and his goons on their way home from school.

CHAPTER 11

MONDAY DAWNED OVER OLD MUSCLE Farm bright, clear, and cool as freshly made lemonade. As the sun drifted in through the blinds in her room, Dominika slowly awoke, listening to her breathing and her heartbeat. *My training is going great, and my driving is getting even better*, she thought, *I love my new family and I know that they love me, but what I don't know is if all of us will survive my trial; oh God, I pray we will.* She sent up a quick prayer on that, and after hearing her sisters getting up and getting ready, Dominika quickly climbed out of bed and pulled out a blue wool top, black leather pants, and black leather high heeled boots that went slightly over her knees. Once it was her turn in the shower, she shined herself up for the day as best she could and got dressed. After putting on some light red lip gloss and black eyeliner, she headed downstairs to join her family for breakfast.

"There is our hot new sister," Dinah announced when Dominika came into the kitchen, "how'd you sleep, Dominika?"

"I slept well, Dinah, thank you," Dominika replied with a small blush.

"Well, it's another school week for us, ladies," Barda told them, for Dominika looked around and was surprised that Ted and Tori weren't around.

"Where are Father and Mother today, sisters," Dominika asked, surprising herself that she was catching onto her new family's southern drawl, with her Russian accent to go along with it.

"They headed to the shop a little early, sis," Kara told her, "some late arrivals, I think; Mom also has to go to the dojo to get it ready for the autumn classes starting soon."

"Though you're a dancer, Dominika, right," Dinah asked.

"I am a dancer, yes," Dominika responded, "Marta and I were dancing before we could talk." She let out a little giggle, which made her sisters burst into giggles also. Dominika got confused, but her sisters told her that her giggle was so adorably cute it was contagious.

"Hehe, well thank you," Dominika replied, blushing again. Just then the clock chimed, and it was time for the Crystals to head out to the garage to select their cars. All four girls were wearing leather boots, pants, and jackets since the day was quite cool outside, but it was their usual style anyway. Kara selected DK, aka Drift King, who was the 1967 Ford Mustang from **THE FAST AND THE FURIOUS: TOKYO DRIFT**, Barda selected Bandit, a 1978 Pontiac Trans Am that was seen at the end of the fourth **FAST AND FURIOUS** film and the beginning of the fifth, Dinah selected Winged Demon, the modified 1969 Dodge Daytona from **FAST AND FURIOUS 6**, while Dominika landed on Toretto, the only true Hemi-powered 1970 Dodge Charger from the first **FAST AND FURIOUS** film. However, before they took off, they did a CB radio check, to make sure they could all hear each other. They all had handles, aka call names. Barda was 'Tough Girl', Kara was 'Fiery Phoenix', Dinah was 'Sexy Siren', Ted was 'Swift Dragon', and Tori was 'Queen Mother'. The family had been thinking of what could Dominika's be, but the girls had chosen it for her, and gotten it approved by their adopted sister. Dominika's handle was 'Dancing Cat', since she was an amazing dancer and when they practiced their fighting skills, she had quick, smooth catlike reflexes. Once the radio check was good and complete, the sisters got their engines roaring on all cylinders and headed off to school.

At the same time, Blohkin and his goons figured the best way to catch Dominika was when she was away from the farm. So, they decided to hide out along the route the girls took from home to school in the afternoon, which would make it a lot less suspicious. *Soon, Dominika Borov,* Blohkin thought, *you'll be right where you belong, in Sparrow School; then when you graduate, I'll personally request that President Putin make you my personal Sparrow.* The Russian agents also decided to not all be in the same vehicle, since that bit them in the rear end pretty hard when they attacked at the farm. So, Blohkin and one of his pals were in one car while the other two were in another. When it was nearly noon, the men got into their positions along the route, and waited.

For the Crystals, the day was pretty much another run-of-the-mill day at school for that time of year. However, when P.E. class came for Dominika, she was thrilled, since they were doing gymnastics. The Russian girl was a natural, and because of her Warrior Princess training, had greatly improved since the last time she'd done gymnastics. The gym teacher was extremely amazed and surprisingly, there was no jealousy among any of the other students. They all were just as amazed as the teacher, and praised Dominika and even asked how she got to be so good at it. When lunch time came, Dominika joined her sisters at their usual table and told them about gym class. Barda, Dinah, and Kara listened, even though they could tell that their adopted sister was heavily blushing. Once Dominika was done, Kara had to speak up.

That is wonderful, Dominika," she told her sister in a praising tone, "but do you realize you're blushing?"

"Oh, sorry," Dominika responded a bit sheepishly, "as I told you when you all took me in, I'm not used to people being nice to me and praising me."

"I remember that, sis," Barda piped up, "but you should welcome that; plus it makes you feel good about yourself, doesn't it?"

"It does, but I fear that will take a long time to get used to it."

"Well, however long it takes, we'll be there always, Dominika," Dinah chimed in, "even if we're not with you physically, we'll be there with you in spirit."

"You will," Dominika gasped.

"Yes," her sisters responded together, "from now on, you'll *never* be alone". That was literal music to Dominika's ears and she literally leaped over the table with an extremely loud, happy squeal and hugged her sisters. The Crystals hugged each other, but not for long, for it was rapidly apparent that the whole cafeteria was dead quiet. Thankfully, the awkwardness only lasted a short time, for the bell tolled and everyone headed off to their afternoon classes.

When the dismissal bell rang at the end of the day, the Crystals walked out to the parking lot, as a group, to get their cars. Once the usual radio check was done, they pulled out and began to head for home, not realizing they'd have to do some fancy maneuvering to shake some very unwanted company before they got home. As they were heading down the main street and had exited the town limits, that was when Dinah, who was last in line, noticed a black sedan pull out of a dirt drive and fall in behind them.

"Breaker, breaker," Dinah called over the CB, "black sedan just pulled out behind us, and it don't look friendly, ladies, comeon."

"Dominika, can you tell if anyone in that car looks familiar to you," Kara called over her CB. Now Dominika was in front of Dinah, yet she could see the car behind her sister and it was gaining fast. It didn't take her long to realize, with horror, who was in the black sedan.

"Oh my god, sisters," Dominika called out, nearly in a scream, "it's Blohkin and his goons!"

"Well then, let's see how well those noodle noggins can drive, shall we ladies," Barda announced. Barda then instructed Kara and herself to move over so that Dominika could take the lead and then her sisters would fall in behind her. As Barda and Kara moved over, Dominika was unsure of what to do then. Though she didn't have to ask.

"Go, Dominika," Dinah called over the CB, "put the pedal down and let it loose!" So, that is exactly what Dominika did, she floored Toretto's gas pedal, got a little startled when the Charger popped a wheelie and took off down the road with a roar and a growl from his supercharged Hemi. When Toretto's front end landed back on the pavement, she felt a sense of calm come over her, as well as determination. *We're going to shake these bastards*, she thought, *if it's the last thing we do*. As she was thinking this, she peeked in her wing mirror and saw Dinah and Winged Demon pulling up and hop in behind her and Toretto. Then, she looked in the rearview mirror and saw that Barda and Kara had positioned DK and Bandit on either side of the road.

Blohkin and his goons were watching this all unfold, but got furious when Barda and Kara positioned their cars on either side of the road.

"Curse those girls," Blohkin growled. He tried going back and forth across the road, but there was no way he was going to get past Barda and Kara. Finally, when he saw that the Crystals were pulling away, since their classic American muscle cars had way more horsepower, he floored his own gas pedal and was finally able to pull off to the shoulder beside Kara and DK. Even though DK had a Nissan Skyline straight six engine with a single turbo, he was still a very fast car. However, when Blohkin tried to get past Kara and DK, they were coming to a bend in the road. Kara could see that the Russian government goons were trying to pull ahead, and she wasn't about to let that happen. She quickly shifted gears, floored the gas, and as she turned DK hard to the right, pulled the modified emergency brake. This caused DK to break into a drift, and his left rear quarter panel whacked Blohkin's sedan, which spun off the shoulder and into the stream that flowed near the road.

"Ladies," Kara called over the CB, "looks like Blohkin and his goons had to stop for a drink." Her sisters all joined in over the CB with laughter, and then fell back into a single file line, with Dominika in front. When the Crystals finally got home, they told their parents about what happened on the way home.

"The time for Dominika's trial is drawing closer then, Mom," Kara asked.

"It is, yes," Tori replied.

"How much longer do you think until it is the time, Honey," Ted asked his wife. He and the girls waited with baited breath.

"At the beginning of next week, Sunday," Tori answered. Ted drew in a loud breath, while the girls all gasped. Dominika however began to cry. Her sisters tried to calm her, but she broke out of their little circle and ran for her room.

"What happens now, Ma," Barda asked.

"We give your sister a little while to let her fear and emotions out, then I'll go and talk with her; the rest of you can get started with your homework." As the triplets headed into the family library, where they usually did their homework, Tori pulled Ted aside.

"I worry for our new daughter, and what she has to face in her trial, my Love."

"I know, Baby, but she is one of us and she has to go through it."

"Yes, hopefully we won't have to get Supertank or the Ripsaw out, but we may not have a choice." Tori was referring to the fully operational, supercharged Sherman tank they owned as well as the little mini tank that had been featured in the movie **FATE OF THE FURIOUS**.

"I don't think so, but they're ready if they're needed," Ted told her, "right now, I think you'd best go comfort Dominika; I'll get started with dinner."

"Thanks, Honey," Tori replied. With that, Ted and Tori hugged each other, then Ted headed to the kitchen to get started on the chicken he was making for dinner while Tori headed upstairs to talk with their newest family member.

CHAPTER 12

In her room, Dominika was kneeling beside her bed, crying her eyes out. When her beautiful sapphire/aquamarine eyes couldn't leak out anymore tears she rose and sat on her bed, took out a mirror from her bedside table's drawer and looked at herself. Her reddish-brown hair was a little messy, but still pretty, and her eyes were still pretty as well, though they were a bit red from crying so hard. *How can I do this*, she thought to herself with a sigh, *even though I've trained, and have some courage, I still feel like I'll fail.* Just then, she thought she saw the image of another person in her mirror. As she stared hard at it, the image moved out of the mirror. Turning quickly, she saw that there was nobody behind her, but when she turned to face front again, she let out a yelp.

Standing in front of her was Xena, her adopted mother's ancestor. Dominika hadn't expected to be able to see Xena since she wasn't a direct descendant of her, and yet here was her adopted mother's ancestor standing before her.

"H-how can I see you, Warrior Queen," the Russian girl asked, "I'm not a blood descendant."

"You're wrong there," Xena told her, "you *do* share my blood."

"What," Dominika gasped in shock, "how, I'm Russian?"

"That is true, but on your father's side of your family is where your connection to me lies; you and your blood sister were meant to come here and find my descendant and her three princesses."

"By your descendant and her three princesses, you mean my adopted mother Tori and her daughters who are my adopted sisters Barda, Dinah, and Kara."

"Yes, dear one; your enemy will come after you everyday this week as you make your way home."

"My enemy meaning Mr. Blohkin, right?"

"Yes; however if you and your adopted sisters stay strong, remember your training, and above all the love your entire family has for each other, you will succeed in your upcoming trial, my descendant." As soon as that was said, Xena vanished. Shortly after, Dominika heard a knock on her door.

"Who is it," she called.

"It's Tori," her adopted mother called, "may I come in, Honey."

"Yes, Mother please do." Tori then came into the room and she and Dominika went over and sat on the bed.

"I wanted to see if you were all right, Honey."

"I'm feeling a little better now." While she was talking, Tori noticed that her adopted daughter seemed to be in the middle of trying to understand something in her head.

"Will you tell me what happened before I came up here, Dominika," she asked softly, "I can tell your thinking about something, and I'd like to help you sort it out, if you'd like." Dominika slowly looked up at her adopted mother, and seeing the love and affection that she had in her mismatched eyes, she swallowed and began.

"I had a visit from your ancestor, Mother," Dominika told her softly.

"Xena," Tori asked.

"Yes, Mother," Dominika replied, "and I didn't think I'd be able to see her since I'm not a direct descendant of hers, but she told me that I am, on my father's side; my birth father that is."

"I had a hunch," Tori said, "or rather Ted, your adopted father, had a hunch."

"You mean, you knew this whole time."

"Yes and no, Honey."

"How?"

"Well, when we adopted you and you began training with your sisters, we, all of us, noticed that you were naturally picking up the techniques of our fighting style, and how well you were able to handle our cars."

"But how could that indicate that I'm related to Xena, Mother?"

"Well, it was earlier today that Ted got some free time in his schedule to look up your family history, and he found that what Xena told you is true, Dominika: you *are* related to her on your father's side."

"Oh my god."

"Honey, I think you need to listen to what ever it is she told you, and plus I think you should share what you learned with your sisters tonight at dinner."

"Yes, Mother, you're right, and I shall."

"That's good to hear, Honey." Just then, they heard Ted ringing the dinner bell, so Tori led Dominika downstairs to the dining area for the evening meal, and so Dominika could reveal what she'd been told to the rest of the family.

CHAPTER 13

WHEN TORI AND DOMINIKA GOT downstairs, they found the triplets and Ted had already gotten the dinner on the table and served. However, they hadn't said grace yet, since two members of the family weren't at the table. So, once all the Crystals were gathered at the table, they all held hands and thanked God for their family, their love, and their food. After their prayer, they all dug in to a lovely dinner of fajitas and soft shell tacos. All through the meal, Dominika chatted happily with her adopted family, yet she was still a little nervous about telling her adopted sisters what Xena had told her, especially the part about learning that Blohkin and his goons would be chasing them home from school all week. She kept trying to convince herself it would be best if she didn't tell them, but in her heart she knew that she loved her new family too much to withhold anything from them, especially if it concerned the safety of her adopted sisters.

Once the main course had been cleared, she asked Ted if she could make an announcement. After her adopted father told her to go ahead, Dominika slowly rose to her feet.

"Mother told me coming downstairs tonight that I should share this with all of you," she began, "and I love you all so much that I have no choice but to agree, and it is this: I saw Xena this afternoon in my bedroom." As she expected, her sisters gasped in shock, but saw that her mother and father didn't.

"How is that possible, Dominika," Dinah asked. Dominika was about to reply when Ted rose to his feet.

"It is possible, everyone, because she is related to Xena on her birth father's side," he explained, "I researched our adopted daughter's family tree earlier this afternoon while you all were still doing your homework." Again Barda, Dinah, and Kara gasped in shock, but the shock turned to joy in about five seconds and they started cheering. However, Dominika said she still had more to tell them, so her sisters quickly quieted down, and their adopted sister continued.

"She also told me that Blohkin is going to be coming after us everyday for the rest of the week on our way home."

"Well then, I think I should have the sheriff and some of the deputies stake out your route," Ted told them, but Dominika and her sisters stopped their father.

"No, Father that is what he'd expect," Dominika told him firmly, "plus Barda, Dinah, Kara, and I feel we must work as a team, and as a family to not let him come anywhere near the farm again."

"The girls are right, Honey," Tori added, "I feel if Dominika is to pass her trial, she must face her enemy along with her sisters."

"Alright then, I trust you girls," Ted agreed, "though try to get an idea of where they're staking out and what kinds of cars they're driving, if you can." Once that was agreed upon, dessert was served, lovely homemade sheet cake. After the table was cleared and the kitchen was cleaned up, Tori, Dominika, and Kara headed out to the barn to check out Kenny and to see how well the old GT40 actually was. Pretty much everything on the car was original from when it had competed at the 1966 24 Hours of LeMans, except for the roll bar, which had been added after the car's namesake, Ken Miles, had been killed testing a different version of the car at Riverside Raceway.

When Dominika and Kara agreed that they both had gotten familiar with where everything was in the cab, they headed back to the house with their mother. Before going to sleep, Dominika joined

Barda, Kara, and Dinah for their usual little ritual they did every night. They stood in a circle and prayed to God for peace, strength, guidance, and protection. They all knew they'd need it this week, though they didn't know that their driving would be pushed almost to it's limit the next several days.

CHAPTER 14

ON TUESDAY WHEN THE CRYSTALS awoke, the girls all gathered in the bathroom to have a talk.

"Well, here we go again, ladies," Barda announced, "another day of school, and another day to shake off that Blohkin bastard and his hitmen."

"Yep, and we're ready for that," Dinah added, "right, sisters?"

"Right," Kara and Dominika answered, though Dominika surprised herself by how confident she sounded. Plus, her adopted sisters were also surprised by how confident and strong she sounded also. After a small group prayer, the girls got about getting ready. Back in her room, Dominika selected a knee-length black leather skirt and a bright blue nylon crop top, throwing her usual little black leather jacket and a pair of shiny over-the-knee high heeled leather boots onto her outfit pile for the day.

Once they'd all showered and dressed for the day, the girls headed downstairs for breakfast. Ted and Tori were already there, with a lovely breakfast of eggs and waffles all laid out.

"Did y'all have a good sleep last night," Ted asked.

"Sure did, Dad," Barda answered first.

"Best ever," Dinah added.

"Fabulous," Kara chimed in.

"Slept like the dead," Dominika finished, letting out a giggle when everyone looked at her with a hint of shock, which in turn made everyone else laugh. As they ate, the family talked about what was going on, and how they might prepare if things with Blohkin and his goons escalated. Even though Ted was still all for getting the police involved, the girls were all flat out against it. So, in an effort to find out, he asked his daughters why they felt that way. Everyone was surprised when it was Dominika who rose to her feet and answered.

"Father, Mother," she began, "I, we, must face our fears and overcome this, and you know that Barda, Dinah, Kara, and I won't be young girls forever; Someday you will have to let us go and we will have to fend for ourselves and face the world on our own one day."

"She's right, Honey," Tori told her husband, "besides they are growing up and will graduate soon." Tori and her daughters all waited as Ted took it in. After a few minutes, he let out a big sigh and got to his feet.

"Y'all are right," he told his family, "you girls are indeed growing up, and will graduate, and I'm very proud of all of you, extremely proud; sometimes it's just hard to let my girls go, but when the time comes, I'll have to, so thanks, Dominika for the reminder."

"You're welcome, Father," Dominika replied, blushing slightly. They all saw that it was time to get ready to head out for the day. The girls helped clear the table and then headed to the barn to get cars. Ted and Tori selected Beach Beast, one of their several Hemi powered 1969 Dodge Daytonas, though before he and his wife headed off to work he did ask the girls if they'd be able to swing by the shop sometime that day. When Barda asked why, their father said that he and Tori felt that they should discuss a few things, and to introduce Dominika to what they all did for a living.

"I'd love to see your business, Father," Dominika replied, "it sounds like it's a great place." Her sisters assured her it was and they told their parents they'd try to swing by at lunch time. Once that was agreed upon, Ted and Tori motored off to Crystal Classics and Customs. The girls decided to go import that day, so Barda selected

Road Missile, the 1997 Mazda RX-7 that was in the first Fast & Furious film. Dinah selected Quick Walker, one of the 1994 Toyota Supras from the first Fast & Furious film, Kara chose Silver Lining, a 2002 Nissan Skyline GT-R, and Dominika settled again on Black Sparrow, a 1972 Nissan Skyline GT-R. After going through their usual radio check, the sisters headed off to school.

When they arrived and parked, they first went to the office to let the principle know that they'd have to leave at around lunch time since their parents needed them at the shop. Dominika was surprised when the principle agreed, but he told her that because of the workload at their parents' business at this time, it was only natural that they'd need the girls there to help out. Once that matter was taken care of, they headed off to homeroom to begin the day. After everyone had taken their seats, Mrs. Bailey announced that the school was holding the annual talent show again on Friday night, and to say that everyone was welcome to attend or perform, whichever they chose. The Crystals and the rest of their classmates only had a short time to dwell on it, for the beginning bell sounded a little bit after that.

The Crystals stayed focused on their studies throughout the morning, and it went well. Dominika had gotten a lot of praise from their art teacher about her drawings in the style of early Russia. However, Barda already knew that, since she and Dominika had art class together and her adopted sister had told her that when they'd first had art class together. Though when Dinah had art class, she seemed sad, since she'd had art class with Dominika's birth sister Marta. Dinah pushed that thought out of her head and focused. It wasn't until lunch time that all four sisters were able to talk about the morning, and what to do for the talent show.

"I've already thought of what we can do, sisters," Dinah announced.

"What," her three sisters asked at the same time.

"We can sing." This caught Barda, Kara, and Dominika by surprise, but only for a few seconds. They burst into legit applause after, though the discussion quickly turned to what should they sing. Kara quickly came up with an idea.

"We each do a solo song, then once all of us have done a solo, we come together and sing a song together," she explained.

"I could do 'Little Deuce Coupe', you know the Beach Boys song," Dinah offered.

"I think I'll do 'Yakity Yak'; that song always cracks me up," Barda joined.

"I'm doing 'Love Story' by Taylor Swift," Kara finished, "it really makes for a nice mood." Then, the triplets looked at Dominika, and wondered what song she should sing for a solo.

"I think I should sing one of my birth mother's songs," Dominika decided, "we did translate her CDs, right?"

"Yeah we got 'em translated to English," Barda told her, "plus, I think that is an awesome idea."

"What should be our group song, sisters," Kara asked. The triplets were surprised when it was Dominika who answered.

"Let's do our fight song: 'Roar' by Katy Perry," she said, adding, "since my trial is going to be the next day." That brought everything home for her adopted sisters, and they agreed that this was the best way to conclude their act. So, once everything was decided, the Crystals quickly put their names down on the sign up sheet.

The afternoon passed pretty quickly, and then the girls headed over to the family business to see what their parents wanted to discuss.

Of course this was Dominika's first time seeing her adopted family's business, and she was quite amazed. As the girls headed through the shop, Dominika was in awe about all the cars that were there getting restored and/ or detailed. Upon reaching the office that was shared by their parents, they entered and greeted their parents with hugs and kisses.

"Hey girls," Ted told them in greeting as he hugged them all, "how was school?"

"It was good, Father," Dominika replied for them, "we put ourselves in the talent show on Friday."

"Yeah, we're going to be singing," Dinah added.

"What will be sung, girls," Tori asked from her desk. Her daughters all told what they'd individually be singing and then finished by saying they were going to finish it all by singing their fight song, since Dominika's trial was the next day. Ted and Tori were greatly thrilled by what their girls were going to do in the talent show, and were glad that they were keeping Dominika's trial in mind. Finally it was Dominika who had to ask why their parents asked them to come to the shop.

"We wanted Barda, Dinah, and Kara to show you what they do to help out here, Honey," Tori replied with a smile. So, with her sisters leading the way, Dominika got a lesson and some hands on time giving completed vehicles a final detail cleaning before being returned to their owners. She was incredibly surprised by how well she picked up what her sisters did to help out, and was even more amazed that she actually enjoyed it as much as they did.

"You're a natural, Dominika," Kara told her after they'd finished their fifth vehicle, a heavily modified 1968 Plymouth Barracuda with a highly custom flame paint job.

"Really," Dominika asked, blushing.

"Totally, sis," Barda joined in.

"Well, thank you then," Dominika replied, blushing harder and giggling. Just then Dinah looked at the clock and announced it was time to head back to the farm.

"Better keep our eyes peeled for Blohkin and his buddies too," she reminded. As the girls got back on the road, Dominika started getting nervous, but somehow she shoved her fear aside and told herself to focus on outrunning and outdriving her enemy. It wasn't until the girls got outside of the town limits that Blohkin and his goons showed themselves. Barda had suggested hitting their nitrous, but Kara had to remind her that Black Sparrow didn't have any, so they had to go to Plan B, which was to do drifting. Now Dominika had worked with her sisters at this and had gotten pretty good at drifting. So, it was much pleasure for all four of them as they slid around the bends while they were laughing as they watched Blohkin and his goons in their rearview mirrors struggle to keep up... again. Finally, at the sharpest curve there was on the trip home, Blohkin and his friends slid off the road and into a mud bog.

"Haha, Crystals 2, Blohkin 0," Dinah laughed over the CB. Barda, Dominika, and Kara joined her and they arrived safely back at the farm five minutes later. Once homework was taken care of, the sisters settled in for a little TV time while they waited for their parents to arrive, which they did about an hour later. Ted and Tori all laughed along with their daughters when they were told of what happened today on the way home with Blohkin and his friends. Ted then suggested that tomorrow they take four of their off-road vehicles. When Dominika asked why, he told the girls that if they came to the shop when school let out, there was a trail that went from behind Crystal Classics and Customs to the farm. Barda, Kara, Dominika, and Dinah all thought that would be awesome, plus Dominika made it even more appealing when she said that Blohkin and his goons would be sitting there all evening wondering when the girls would show themselves. Tori then asked if Blohkin would wonder if there was another route from town to the farm. Ted told her that if someone looked at a road map, there was only one way to get from Old Muscle Farm to town, and that the trail wasn't visible from the parking lot and street area near the shop.

"So basically what you're saying, Father," Dominika asked, trying to figure it out, "is that now my sisters and I can get from home to town without Blohkin even seeing us?"

"Exactly, Honey," Ted told her.

"Awesome," all four girls cheered. Then the family got dinner started, a nice feast of homemade fajitas with a toppings buffet. When the evening meal was done, and everything was cleaned up, the girls headed up to get some sleep. Even though they knew it was a bit of a gamble, they had no idea that it would play out the next day just as they figured. In fact, it was even better then they figured.

CHAPTER 15

WEDNESDAY DAWNED BRIGHT AND SUNNY as fresh made lemonade, and the Crystal girls awoke feeling pumped and energized, especially Dominika. Once they'd all showered and gotten dressed, with each wearing leather in some way as well as all wearing sexy leather high heeled boots, the sisters headed down to breakfast, to which they were greeted by their parents who'd made their favorite, Mountain Man Breakfast. As the family ate, the girls discussed how their outfits for the talent show should be. Tori suggested they all wear what they felt the most beautiful in, and Ted agreed. After they each discussed the leather ensemble they'd wear, Barda suggested that since the song they'd all be singing together at the end was their fight song, that they wear their Warrior Princess outfits.

"I don't know if that is a good idea, Barda," Tori said, "I don't want you girls to expose that side of our family."

"Mom, we won't really be doing that," Dinah insisted, "the folks at school will just think that we're wearing costumes that go with the song."

"Plus, we haven't told anyone at school about our heritage, or that **ROAR** is our fight song," Kara finished.

"The girls do have a point there, Honey," Ted told his wife, "besides I think it would be awesome to see our princesses showing their true colors, but not actually telling." Tori agreed to it then, and looking at the clock, it was time for the family to head out for the day. As usual, Ted and Tori left first, though not before reminding the girls about their plan to make Blohkin and his goons look like total idiots. Once their parents were off to work at the shop, Barda, Dinah, Kara, and Dominika selected the off road rides they'd take. Dominika chose Dirt Devil, a 1970 Dodge Charger, Dinah chose Dirt Challenge, a 2011 Dodge Challenger, Barda chose Zee Dirt, a 1968 Chevrolet Camaro, and Kara chose Rallye Fighter. Once they'd all climbed in, strapped in, and run through the usual radio check, the sisters headed off to school.

The school day was mostly uneventful in the morning, and at lunch, the Crystals chatted happily about their singing performance at the talent show on Friday, and how they'd make Blohkin and his trained goons look like total dim-witted fools later in the afternoon.

"Sisters, I just realized something that may make this even more sweet," Kara told them.

"What," her sisters asked together, which made them all blush, Dominika most.

"Blohkin and his goons are always on the same side of the road, which will put their backside to the trail we'll be on this afternoon."

"Oh my gosh," Barda gasped through her laughter, "now we'll *really* make him and his friends look like idiots."

"Oh yes," Dominika said, "this is going to be amazing."

"Plus," Dinah chimed in, " I just did a map search of the area, and discovered something else as well."

"What?"

"The brush and trees are thick enough that it will muffle the sound of our engines; in addition, we'll be able to see them, but they have no chance at all of seeing us." This made the sisters laugh even more, but what really sent them into nearly hysterical laughter was the fact that they could go at any speed they wanted, since there were no speed limits off road.

"I can't wait for this, sisters," Dominika told them once they'd stopped laughing enough to breath, "and thank you again."

"Aww, you're welcome, Dominika," Barda told her sweetly, giving her a one arm hug around the shoulders, "that's what family does; plus we're never goin' to leave you in the dust on your own."

"That's true," Kara added, "we were raised to help others in need, whether it's our own family or someone else in town."

"And we *always* stick together and have each other's backs," Dinah finished. They noticed it was nearly time for the bell, but before it rang, the sisters put their fists together, and asked Dominika to join them. At first, their adopted sister was a little confused, but since she was one of them now, she added her fist to the circle. The sisters then recited their own little chant that they'd come up with after they'd all gone through their trials: "Warriors united, future queens eternally." Right as they finished their chant, the bell rang. The rest of the school day went by like a normal day, though one of Kara's classmates, Holly, got sent to the office because she was having a video call with another girl while everyone else was taking a quiz. Once the day was done, the Crystals headed out to get their vehicles.

CHAPTER 16

ONCE THE CRYSTALS HAD GOTTEN their vehicles fired up, and had gone through their usual radio check, they headed for the family business. On the way, Kara called ahead on the CB to let their parents know they were headed over, and to show them where the access to the trail was in the back lot. Ted responded that he would, since Tori was busy with scheduling. After signing off, they maintained radio silence, since they didn't want to risk tipping off Blohkin and his goons. Another five minutes went by before they saw Crystal Classics and Customs ahead of them.

As they pulled into the parking lot, they saw their father waving them over by the gate that led around back to where customers vehicles were brought into the shop. After closing the front gate, Ted hopped into a little custom golf cart that looked like a '57 Chevrolet Bel Air, and motioned for his daughters to follow him towards the back of the back lot behind the building. Dominika, who was in Dirt Devil and behind Barda who was in Zee Dirt, was a little nervous and voiced it. However, Dinah, who was behind her in Dirt Challenge, told her to just allow her self to feel free and able to go as fast as she wished, since there are no speed limits on dirt. It was right after this was said that Ted opened a back gate that led out onto the trail. Kara, who was in front in Rallye Fighter, hit the gas pedal and took off through the gate. Barda and Zee Dirt were close behind. At last Dominika and Dirt Devil were up. She closed her eyes for a brief minute, and in her mind's eye, she heard her birth family come to her and tell her to go for it and to feel free. And as quick as a horse spooked by a rattlesnake, Dominika opened her sapphire/aquamarine eyes and floored Dirt Devil's throttle and took off through the gate and down the trail, followed by Dinah in Dirt Challenge.

Out on the trail, flying through the woods at break neck speed, Dominika realized she truly did feel free, and was more amazed at how well she was able to keep up with her sisters and to keep from running Dirt Devil into the trees. *This is one of the most incredible days of my life*, she thought, *I'm glad that we are going to pause and see how Blohkin and his goons feel when we don't show on the road.* To confirm that her mind reading ability was correct, she saw Kara and Barda bring their vehicles to a halt, so she hit her own brakes and Dinah followed suit. They left their engines running, but they all climbed out of their top hatches and Barda took out a pair of binoculars.

"Girls, I can see that knucklehead and his goonies from here," she called quietly.

"How do they look, Barda," Dominika asked. Barda took a good long look before responding.

"Haha, they look like a bunch of canceled stamps, Dominika."

"Oh man, this worked like a charm," Dinah chimed in.

"For sure," Kara concluded, "we'll have to thank Dad for this idea." She then told them they'd better get going, so they all slid back down into their cabs and took off for the farm. Meanwhile, back out at the roadside, Blohkin and his friends really were feeling like a bunch of canceled stamps. As they started arguing and fuming among themselves, Blohkin's phone rang. He looked at it and told everyone to shut up, for President Putin was calling. Upon answering, the Russian president wanted to know if he'd caught Dominika yet.

"Not yet, Mr. President," Blohkin replied, "but I'm close."

"Well, hopefully you and your friends can catch her," Putin told him, "for I expect her to be brought home, and put into State School Four before the beginning of the New Year; do you understand?"

"Yes, Mr. President," Blohkin answered. After hanging up, he and his friends headed back to their motel to figure out what should their next step be, and to vent out their frustrations.

Dominika and her sisters were already back at the farm, and had gotten their vehicles stashed in the barn before Blohkin and his friends had even gotten back to town, since by going flat out through the woods they could travel faster then by the main road. After getting their backpacks into the house, they sat down to catch their breath, for they'd been running on a huge adrenaline wave, and had been hysterically laughing about how they'd made complete idiots out of Blohkin and his friends.

"I sure wish we could see how those idiots looked when we never showed on the road," Dinah laughed.

"You can say that again, sis," Barda joined in, "I bet they're feeling worse then a fox that was outfoxed by it's own prey."

"I can't believe we got away with that," Dominika added, "not to mention getting past Blohkin and his friends without them seeing us." Kara eventually calmed her sisters down and they got their homework out of the way.

A little while later, Tori and Ted got home from the shop and asked how it went with taking the trail home instead of the main road. Dominika told them how her birth family seemed to come to her in spirit and told her to just let herself be free, and how free it felt to just be flying through the woods at over seventy miles per hour with her sisters around her. Plus, they all burst out laughing when they started thinking of how Blohkin and his goons must be feeling about not seeing them come along the main road after school.

"Father, thank you for showing us the trail," Dominika said, "now we can travel home without having to worry about Blohkin."

"I wouldn't get too excited just yet, Honey," Ted told her, "there is always the possibility that he and his goons could get wise or that someone could squeal on you girls; so keep taking the trail home, but keep your guards up, your ears on, and your eyes peeled."

"Sure thing, Dad," the girls all said at the same time, making them all blush and laugh. After a wonderful dinner of turkey strips and mashed potatoes, the sisters headed upstairs. Once they went through their evening ritual to draw strength and protection for the day ahead, the family retired for the night.

Meanwhile, at the motel, Blohkin and his friends had vented their frustrations, and he'd gathered them together.

"How could those girls outsmart us," one of his friends asked.

"Yeah," said another, "we were so hidden on the side of the road there is no way we could've missed them."

"I don't know, guys," Blohkin told them, "but we have to get Dominika and get her back to Russia for the president; she is to be his new sparrow, and she *must* be put through State School Four as soon as possible." Blohkin went on to tell them they stick to the plan, and if they hadn't caught her by Friday, then they'd have to take it up a notch. Satisfied, he and his goons turned in for the night, not knowing that they'd keep being thwarted by the Crystals, and that they'd be playing right into Dominika becoming secret royalty along with her new family.

CHAPTER 17

ON THURSDAY, IT WAS DOMINIKA'S turn to do dawn patrol, though Dinah went with her to show what they did while out on dawn patrol. Riding along in Pete, a modified Peterbilt from the spin off movie **HOBBS & SHAW**, they fixed a few broken fence posts and caught a few armadillos that were trying to sneak into the vegetable patches. As they were heading back toward the barn to stash Pete, Dinah felt the urge to talk to her adopted sister.

"Are you still feeling nervous about your trial, Dominika," she asked.

"Yes, Dinah, very much so," Dominika replied. However, Dinah could see that Dominika had something else on her mind, and knew she had to get her sister to open up about it.

"Is there something else you're worried about, sis?"

"I worry about losing you, as well as Barda and Kara, and Father and Mother."

"Aww don't worry about us, sis, we won't abandon you, ever."

"I know, but I can't help it."

"It is understandable, Dominika; when Barda, Kara, and myself had our trials, we were scared too, though I think mine was tougher then Barda's and Kara's."

"How so, Dinah?"

"I was totally and completely on my own." And Dinah told Dominika about her trial, which involved her escaping from an ocean liner where the captain and crew were sacrificing female passengers to the devil. Then, after she'd sunk the ship and escaped in a lifeboat, she'd been attacked by a shark, but had killed it before it could kill her. She was nearly dead by the time the rest of the family finally located her with their old B-17 bomber and rescued her.

"That was the most scared I've ever been in my life, Dominika," Dinah finished, "but I survived, and I'm a Warrior Princess like my sisters."

"I'm glad you survived, Dinah," Dominika told her sister, "you, as well as Barda and Kara, have truly helped me through what I'm dealing with." However, Dinah could tell that there still was something on Dominika's mind, and had to get her sister to open up about it. So, when they got Pete back in his stall and were heading in for breakfast, she asked Dominika if there was anything else she wanted to discuss before getting ready for school.

"Remember when I saw your ancestor Xena," Dominika asked quietly. Dinah nodded.

"I remember, Dominika," she exclaimed, "and you were quite shocked about it."

"Mother came into my room right after Xena vanished and told me that Father looked up my ancestry and said that what Xena told me about my father being a descendant of hers; I actually looked it up and it is true."

"That is incredible, sis."

"I know, but I think I'm more shocked then you are." Just then, the rest of the family came into the kitchen and Dinah retold everything that Dominika had said. Naturally, everyone was astounded, but it made sense, especially to Barda and Kara, since they'd told Dominika that she was mastering their fighting techniques so quickly.

"Its no wonder she was, girls," Tori told them, "Dominika shares our blood."

"Yes, I do," Dominika told everyone, "and because I do, I want to make breakfast this morning." She explained that in her homeland they would make food for people as a sign of hospitality. While her adopted family waited at the table, Dominika mixed up some small Russian breakfast buns. Once everything was served, the family dug in. Everyone was delighted with the buns, which did cause Dominika to blush, but she was happy that her new family loved something that she'd learned from her old family. In fact, she saw her birth parents and her birth sister standing off to one side, smiling happily at her.

All too soon it was time to head out for the day. Dominika wanted to take the trail to school, but her family told her it would be better if they went by way of the main road, so it looked normal. The girls were going to use the same cars they'd used yesterday, though for going to work, Ted and Tori decided to use Red Skull instead of the General Lee. Now, Red Skull was a look-alike to the General, but in a more creepy way. The Charger was painted matte black, and had the '01' and Rebel flag painted in bright red. What made him creepy was the skull in the middle of the zero on the doors and the skulls instead of stars on the Rebel flag painted on the roof. Plus, Red Skull had a Dodge Viper V10 engine, an auxiliary fuel cell in the trunk, and two nitrous canisters in the back seat. Sometimes, people called Red Skull "the General Lee's evil twin". Dominika asked her adopted parents why, and they told her that if Blohkin and his goons wanted to target them, they could outrun him better. This gave Dominika some comfort, for she wanted nothing to happen to her adoptive family, even though it seemed that during her upcoming trial something would.

After the girls had left, Ted and Tori headed off to work. As they were heading toward town, Ted noticed a dented Lincoln Town Car pull out of a narrow lane. Looking closer into the rearview mirror, he saw that it was Blohkin and his goons.

"Babe, we got company," he told Tori. Tori looked behind them and gasped, but quickly regained her composure.

"So they *did* decide to try and come after us," she replied.

"Anything you wish me to do, my Queen?"

"Smoke 'em."

"With pleasure." At that, Ted mashed Red Skull's pedal to the metal. Blohkin and his goons tried to follow, but their banged up Town Car couldn't compete with the Crystals' Charger's speed. Coming around a corner, Ted hit the nitrous button, and Red Skull shot ahead as if the Charger had been shot out of a cannon. Unfortunately for Blohkin and his goons, they spun out of control and whipped a tree in the side. They were all okay, but they were furious. So, they quickly got their car back on the road and headed back to their motel and wait for school to let out and try to catch the girls again.

Meanwhile, Ted and Tori had shut off Red Skull's nitrous and were pulling in to the shop. As they greeted everyone on the morning shift and headed for their office, they knew that they had to tell the girls to take the trail home, and to be careful. So, Tori went ahead and called the school.

At school, the Crystal siblings were called to the guidance office. When Barda, Dinah, Kara, and Dominika were told what happened to their parents, Dominika broke down crying. The guidance counselor, Ms. Morgan, and her sisters tried to calm her down, but the Russian girl shook them off and ran out of the office, still sobbing.

"Is she going to be alright, girls," Ms. Morgan asked.

"I think we know where she's going," Kara told her, "we'll go find her." With that, Dominika's adopted sisters headed out to the enclosed courtyard, and found her crying under a large cedar tree near the little koi pond. Dominika heard them approaching and looked up, her beautiful sapphire/aquamarine eyes still wet with tears.

"Is it okay if we sit with you, Dominika," Kara asked. Dominika hiccupped, but nodded. Barda handed her a handkerchief from her pocket while Dinah and Kara hugged her. After a few minutes, Dominika spoke.

"Thank you, sisters," she told them with a sniffle, "I know I shouldn't have acted that way, but I couldn't help it."

"It's understandable, Dominika," Dinah told her softly, "I was nearly ready to scream myself."

"Y-you were, Dinah," Dominika asked.

"I could tell she was," Barda chimed in, "I'm thankful you didn't, though." Barda went on to tell that sometimes when Dinah screamed with intense emotion, glass would sometimes shatter. Dominika asked Dinah if this was true, and Dinah confirmed it was, blushing since it was a bit embarrassing. It was then that Dominika remembered something when she'd been taken in by the Crystals, something that didn't seem like it was normal, and she had to ask Kara.

"Kara, do you remember when you and the others found me in your car's trunk," she asked.

"How can we forget when we found you in the General's trunk, looking half dead," Kara replied, shuddering slightly at the memory.

"I'd had a bullet graze my calf, but I don't have a scar; how is that possible?"

"It's because I healed you, Dominika."

"Healed me, how?"

"With my hands."

"How is that possible?"

"It is my special gift, sis, we all have one, including you." Kara went on to explain how each member of the family had a 'special ability'. Ted was a psychic, Tori could see the future, Kara was a healer, Barda was an empath as well as abnormally strong, and Dinah could manipulate the environment with her emotions. Of course, Dominika was a mind reader, so she knew that her adopted sisters were gifted individuals, but hadn't explored it in depth, until now. However, the bell rang and the Crystals all hurried back inside, so they wouldn't be late for class.

The rest of the day passed by without further incident, and Dominika actually got a high score in art class for an oil pastel painting she'd done of her family. When the day was over, the girls headed for their cars. Dominika had stashed her painting in a safe way in order to get it home, though she still worried about it. After they got their cars fired up, and had done their usual CB check, they headed for the shop. *I hope Mother and Father like my painting,* Dominika thought, *and hopefully when my trial happens, nothing will happen to Mother, Father, or my sisters.* When the girls arrived, they parked behind the fence, where Ted and Tori had parked Red Skull when they'd arrived that morning. Their parents came out to greet them, and Dominika nearly knocked them both off their feet, mainly because she was so relieved to see them.

"I'm so happy that Blohkin and his goons didn't hurt you," she told them, with a small sob escaping her throat. Ted and Tori hugged their adopted daughter and gently kissed her. Barda, Dinah, and Kara joined in the hug also. When they pulled apart, Dominika told Ted and Tori that she had something for them. Running back over to Dirt Devil, she pulled out the portfolio that held her painting. Looking at it quickly, she was relieved that it had made it unscathed. Running back over to her family, she handed it to her adoptive parents and told them to open it. When they did, Ted and Tori were surprised and hugged Dominika.

"Thank you, Honey," Tori told her, "we'll hang this in the waiting area, so everyone who comes to the shop can see it."

"It'll be a nice addition to the other art from your sisters we have in there," Ted added. Her sisters told Dominika that a lot of their own art was on display in the waiting room at the shop. Dominika wanted to look, but her family said they'd best get home safely. She was a little sad, but was willing to wait. After getting back in their cars, Ted opened the gate to the trail, and the girls took off down it. As she and her sisters raced through the woods, Dominika felt her birth family riding along with her. *Stop worrying, Honey*, her birth mother said, *enjoy your new life with your new family; we may not physically be with you anymore, but we're always here in spirit.* Plus, she heard Marta add to the conversation, *You won't be able to complete your trial if you keep getting these bouts of fear and sadness; you have to trust what they've taught you, what our ancestor passed down to you through blood.* At that instant, Dominika knew she *had* to trust her instincts, which were telling her to let go of her fear, and flying through the woods in Dirt Devil, with her family, she knew that she could do that. She let her adrenaline take over, and as they neared the farm, let out a "Whoo" along with her sisters.

As the girls pulled into the farm, they all hopped down from their vehicles and gave each other a high ten. Once their heart rates slowed down, they pulled into the barn one by one and got their vehicles stashed back in their stalls. Just as they were leaving the barn, their parents came charging in from the trail with Red Skull.

Ted and Tori had closed up at the shop, and Ted had gotten Tori to bring Red Skull into the back area to where the hidden entrance to the trail was. Once he'd finished getting the shop secure and shut down, he headed out back to join his wife and to get the gate open. Tori pulled the Charger onto the trail, then climbed out of the window, swung over the roof and into the shotgun window, as Ted got the gate closed and secured then jumped in through the driver's window. After he and his wife were strapped in, Ted gunned Red Skull's Viper engine and they charged down the trail. As they passed by the main road, they saw Blohkin and his goons, but they didn't see Ted and Tori. When they charged into the front yard at the farm, they saw their daughters coming out of the barn. Tori and Ted climbed out of Red Skull and hugged their daughters.

"Was Red Skull alright on the trail, Father," Dominika asked.

"Ahh sure," Ted answered, as if it was nothing, "he can ride trails just as good as the General, only Red Skull has more horsepower, and the nitrous." Tori asked Dinah if she wouldn't mind getting Red Skull back in his stall, and Dinah agreed, since she loved Chrysler products, like her dad. Barda and Kara headed inside, and Dominika started to follow when Ted asked her if she'd stay back a minute. After Dinah headed inside to join Barda and Kara, Tori and Ted led Dominika over to one of the stalls that looked almost like a bank vault.

"Sweetheart, did your sisters tell you what happened on our way to work this morning," Tori asked.

"Yes Mother, they did," Dominika replied, "and it made me cry."

"I'm sorry to hear that it brought you to tears, Honey," Ted went on, "but I know your sisters cheered you up."

"Yes Father, they did, and I'm thankful to them for that." She then asked why they wished to speak to her privately. Her adoptive parents looked at one another and then turned back to their adopted daughter.

"Blohkin and his goons read Red Skull's license plate number, Dominika," Tori answered slowly. Dominika gasped, and Tori and Ted could see that their adopted daughter was starting to cry again.

Quickly they wrapped her in a group hug, which calmed her some, but she was still nervous.

"Then that means he and his goons can find us," Dominika whimpered.

"Yes, but I have an idea on how to scare him and his goons off until we want them to come onto our property," Ted told her.

"How, Father?"

"Well, it involves what is in this very secure stall."

"What is in there, exactly?"

"Literally the most evil car we own, Dominika." Ted shown a light at the name on the stall, and it made Dominika gasp: CHRISTINE. She'd heard about the story, but had only thought it was just a story. Ted went on to tell her the same thing he'd told Tori about how Christine had come to the farm, that it had been a quiet night with no out of the ordinary sounds. Then, when Ted was heading over to the barn the next morning, there she was parked in the driveway. Her adoptive parents opened a small window in the stall door, and let their adopted daughter take a look at the evil Plymouth Fury, and the sight of her sent heavy shivers up Dominika's spine.

"H-h-how are we going to be able to make her do as she's told," Dominika asked nervously.

"Leave that to me, Dushka," Ted answered, "I'm the only one who knows how to get that four wheeled fiend to actually follow orders." So, as Tori lead Dominika back to the house to join her sisters, Ted headed into the stall and gave the evil Plymouth her marching orders.

Meanwhile, back at their motel, Blohkin and his gang were making plans to attack the Crystals on their farm that night. Little did they know that they wouldn't be grabbing Dominika that night, nor that they'd be chased back to the motel only after barely escaping becoming roadkill by a driverless car.

CHAPTER 18

At around 11:00 that night, Blohkin and his goons snuck onto the Crystals' property. As they crept into the main barnyard area and were coming past the R&R (Repair & Restoration) shed and the barn, they heard 1950s American music playing.

"I thought they were all asleep," one of Blohkin's friends whispered.

"Maybe they decided to stay out and enjoy the stars," Blohkin replied quietly, "the perfect mistake; first though, we'd better find out where that music is coming from." As they crept around the barn, they realized that the music was coming from a red and white 1958 Plymouth parked in the middle of the driveway.

"Maybe she brought a boy over and they're having sex in the back," another of Blohkin's friends said.

"Yeah, perfect chance to get a look at how big her breasts are," added another.

"Shut up, you idiots," Blohkin whispered harshly, "she'll hear us." He then got out his cell phone and was about to make a call to the Russian president. Right as he was doing this, they heard the car start. They got ready to dash at the car, but paused when they realized something wasn't quite right. The car was running, the radio was playing, but they couldn't see anyone inside the car. Right when they quietly acknowledged this, the headlights came on, high beam, and the engine revved and the car charged at them!

"Scatter," Blohkin yelled. He and his friends tried, but it seemed no matter what way they ran, that Plymouth was always right there. As they kept running around like chickens with their heads chopped off, Blohkin and his fellow agents were getting more and more terrified. *This absolutely can't be happening*, Blohkin thought, *this is like a horror film.* Still, he knew, and his friends knew, this was no horror film and it actually was happening.

Soon, they were all able to make it back to their car, but the driverless Plymouth wasn't finished. It rammed the side where the gas tank was, as well as taking a good sized chunk out of the front end. Fortunately, they were able to get their car going. As they made their exit, they looked back and saw the Plymouth coming after them. However, what was *really* scaring them was watching as the driverless Plymouth fixed itself right before their eyes. Soon, they saw the exit of the driveway, and gunned their car out onto the main road and took off. They were relieved when they saw that the Plymouth wasn't following them.

Meanwhile, back Old Muscle Farm, Tori and Ted got Christine back into her stall, and secured her in it.

"Beautiful work, you fine, finned fiend," Ted told the evil Plymouth, "glad to see you've learned that I'm in charge around here." After getting the barn secured for the night, Tori and Ted headed inside and up to bed. They discussed what they'd heard Blohkin and his goons talking about, and how gross it sounded. They both knew that they'd had sex in the back of several of their cars, but *Never* in Christine, knowing the evil Plymouth would try to do something.

"Should we show the girls the surveillance videos tomorrow," Tori asked her husband.

"Why the heck not, Baby," Ted told his wife, "besides Dominika will get a kick out of seeing them running around like a bunch of headless chickens." They both had a good laugh over that, but then Tori got serious and told her husband that there was a chance that Blohkin and his goons could call for reinforcements. Ted informed her that when the sheriff had interviewed Dominika before she and him had gone back in time to retrieve Marta's body, she'd told the sheriff Blohkin's phone number, and that the sheriff had passed that information along to the state government.

"If he does try to send a call for extra men or equipment, all he'll get will be an American facility, and they'll be reporting him and his goons."

"What about calling the Russian government?"

"That could be trickier, especially since he's quite close with Mr. Pinhead, aka "president" Putin; so we'll just have to hope for the best on that, but it might be easier to make that complicated for him."

"How, Honey?"

"Keep ahold of his means of communication, Darling." Ted then reached into the pocket of the shorts he'd been wearing and pulled out a cell phone. He said he'd found it on the ground after Blohkin and his goons had been chased off, and it had been right by where Blohkin had been standing and had been about to make a quick call.

"Ted, you're a genius," Tori gasped, hugging her husband.

"Thanks, Tori," he answered with a chuckle, "just have to get the sheriff and one of his IT guys out here tomorrow and see if we can't work a little magic." After a another hug and kiss, Tori and Ted snuggled close together under the blankets and went to sleep for the night.

By this time, Blohkin and his goons had gotten back to their motel. As they raced into their room, locking and bolting the door, they took stock of what had happened.

"What was that," one of the agents asked.

"I don't know," Blohkin answered, "but they made fools out of us, and that is *not* something we forgive on."

"I think we may have to make an exception this time, Blohkin," another fellow agent told him.

"Why is that!?"

"How do you explain us being chased around a barnyard by a driverless car that fixes itself also?"

"Exactly, how to you fight and defend against something that can't possibly be alive?"

"Shut up, all of you," Blohkin yelled, shocking the room into quiet, "just go to sleep and we'll regroup in the morning." He then stormed into the bathroom and slammed the door. As they all got ready for bed, Blohkin wondered how he and his fellow Russian agents could get back at the Crystals for stopping them, **AGAIN**, from reaching their objective. While his friends got ready to turn in themselves, Blohkin slowly went to sleep thinking of how he'd rough up Dominika before she even got into Sparrow School, and also wondered if the president would allow him to have her for a few nights after she got out. He was so obsessed with all his planning, he never bothered to check to see if he still had his phone with him. Which would turn out to be a not so good plan...

CHAPTER 19

On Friday morning, Kara had dawn patrol, but the others woke up along with her. After they'd all showered and gotten dressed, with at least one leather clothing item other then their high heeled boots, Dinah, Barda, and Dominika were all gathered at the kitchen table. It was a professional day that day for the teachers, so the students didn't have school, though they would be going back to the school that evening for the talent show. The girls were going over what they'd sing and what they'd wear, even though they knew for when they'd all sing Roar together, they'd be wearing their warrior princess outfits. Dominika was still a little nervous, since she hadn't had her trial yet, but her sisters were still telling her not to worry.

Soon Kara joined them, having stashed Pete back in the barn, and they were still going over their plans for that evening when their parents came in.

"Girls," Ted announced, "we have something to share with y'all."

"What," the girls all asked at the same time, causing them to blush and giggle like their mom.

"Blohkin and his goons came on our property last night," Tori said slowly. The girls all gasped, except Dominika who let out a yelping "no". Everyone quickly hugged her tightly before she got too emotional. Once she'd calmed, Tori and Ted told them that they'd set Christine against Blohkin and his goons, and she had quite literally scared them silly. They then showed their daughters the security footage, and everyone burst out laughing at how stupid Blohkin and his goons looked running around the barnyard like a bunch of headless chickens. Even Dominika laughed, so hard in fact that she started crying, but they were tears of mirth, not sadness. Their parents then asked if they were going to practice their songs, and the girls said they were, so they headed downstairs. Though when they got to their little karaoke area, Dominika realized that she hadn't selected which song of her birth mother's to sing. Quickly looking through the song titles, she found, to her, the perfect one: Sparrows in the Spring. It had been her favorite when she was younger, and since it told of the freedom of birds in nature, and that she was fighting for her freedom in order to not be forced to become a Sparrow, she knew that it was the perfect song of her birth mother's to sing at the talent show. Once her song was selected, Dominika and her sisters practiced all day.

At around 3:30, the Crystals piled into Fast Feline, a red 2016 Dodge Charger Hellcat, and headed for the school. Upon arrival, Tori and Ted headed into the auditorium while their daughters headed backstage to get ready. All four of the sisters wore black leather high heeled boots, but their leather outfits were different styles and colors. Kara wore a long hot pink leather dress, Barda wore a yellow turtleneck top and red leather pants, Dinah wore a red leather crop top and a short blue leather skirt. Finally, Dominika emerged in a long, tight black leather tube dress as well as a pair of black leather opera gloves. Her sisters were amazed and gave her a round of applause.

"Wow, Dominika," Barda told her, "you're the hottest looking out of all of us."

"Thank you, Barda," Dominika replied, giggling and blushing, "it was one of my mother's old stage outfits." Her sisters felt it was a wonderful touch, singing one of her birth mother's best songs, wearing one of the costumes she'd worn onstage. They all then made sure they'd remembered their Warrior Princess outfits, minus their tiaras since Dominika didn't yet have one. Upon making sure that everything was in order for their group song, they headed over to the main waiting area backstage for their turn.

CHAPTER 20

Soon, it was time for the Crystals to start. Barda went out first, and had their fellow students laughing and some parents frowning when she sang 'Yakity Yak'. Once she bowed off, Dinah took her place and gave a very fine rendition of 'Little Deuce Coupe'. She blew a few kisses and then it was Kara's turn to perform 'Love Story'. The audience was enchanted by how she sang it, and she got a huge applause when she was finished. After curtsying, she came backstage and received hugs from her sisters.

"Alright, Dominika," Dinah said, "you're on."

"Good luck, sis," Kara added, giving Dominika a quick kiss on the cheek. Dominika then hugged all three of her sisters and headed out onstage. The audience was awestruck when Dominika emerged, which made her a little nervous. Though, seeing her sisters off to the side relieved that fear.

"Good evening," she began, "I'm Dominika Crystal, and this is a song that my birth mother, Irina Borov, wrote and performed back in Russia; I hope you enjoy my singing of her hit song 'Sparrows in the Spring'." Then the music started and she started to sing. The audience was amazed at how well Dominika's voice rang out, displaying her emotion and her love for her birth family by singing this song. Even her adopted sisters were reduced to tears at the depth of emotion Dominika displayed.

When she finished singing, Dominika looked out over the audience and there was literally silence. At that instant, Dominika froze with fear, and she started to quiver. However, the audience broke into a literal standing ovation for her, and even her adopted sisters ran out onstage and hugged her. After breaking free of her sisters, Dominika gave a bow along with Barda, Dinah, and Kara.

"Don't go away," Dominika told the audience, "we're not done yet." The sisters then ran backstage and quickly changed out of their sexy leather outfits and put on their Warrior Princess outfits. Then, after doing a quick change of music, they headed out onstage for their group performance of 'Roar'. They let Dominika take the main vocals while Barda, Dinah, and Kara were the backup vocals. When they got to the part of the song where Katy Perry did multiple roars, which totaled five, they each did one roar and then for the final, all four of them roared. It was quite a shock, for it felt like the whole building shook when they all did the final roar. Then, all of their voices, with Dominika's being the loudest, rang out the final refrain.

When the song was over, they got a standing ovation. As Dominika did a group bow with her sisters, she saw her adopted parents, Tori and Ted, standing near the front, happily applauding. Then, as she turned to head backstage, she saw her birth family applauding as well. Also, her birth mother, Irina, whispered, *beautiful performance.*

After another hour, it was time to announce who'd taken first, second, and third prize. They started with the third prize winner, Tommy Hamilton, for his amazing magic tricks. Second prize went to Holly Anderson, for her gymnastics skills. Finally, first prize went to the Crystal siblings, for their amazing singing. As she joined her sisters onstage, Dominika could hardly see through her tears of joy. After they'd gotten their prize and had their picture taken for the yearbook, the sisters ran backstage to change back into their regular clothes, stashed their Warrior Princess outfits as well as their solo outfits in their duffel bags, and then ran back out to the school lobby to meet their parents.

When the sisters found their parents, they gathered together for a big group hug. The family headed out to where they'd left Fast Feline and began to head home. Though after they'd gotten outside of the town limits, Ted spoke up.

"Don't forget, everyone, that Dominika's trial is tomorrow." This, of course made everyone nervous, Dominika especially. Thanks to her mind reading ability, she sensed everyone telling her not to worry, but she still couldn't totally shake the feeling that something was going to happen to her adopted family. However, she found herself feeling more confident in herself, mainly thanks to her adopted family showing her so much love and encouragement. When they got home, and had stashed Fast Feline back in the barn, Tori and Ted asked the girls to come to the track. They were all confused, but followed suit. Once there, Dominika noticed something low to the ground covered with a tarp. Tori pulled the tarp off, revealing Kenny, Ken Miles' GT40, but told everyone to take a look at the top of the driver's side door.

"Dominika, your name is written here, along with other names," Kara exclaimed. Dominika looked, and sure enough, under the names of Ken Miles, Lloyd Ruby, and Dennis Hulme, was her name. Ted then told her that it had been his idea. Dominika hugged her adoptive father, sobbing tears of joy.

"Thank you, Father," she said, hiccupping slightly.

"Don't thank me yet," Ted replied, "open the door." Dominika opened the door, and found a driver's suit inside. Looking it over, she found it was fire resistant, tight fitting leather, which is how her sisters liked their driver's suits. Then, Dominika started happily crying more when she saw her name, Dominika Crystal, sewn on the left breast pocket.

"Go ahead, Honey," Tori told her, indicating the helmet inside, "take a few hot laps." Dominika didn't have to be told twice. Grabbing the helmet and strapping it on, she jumped into the old Ford, fired him up, and took off.

As she guided Kenny around the track, Dominika felt more at one with the old GT40 then she had felt with any of the other vehicles she'd driven, with the exception of Black Sparrow, the 1972 Nissan Skyline GT-R from the movie **FAST FIVE**. She periodically checked the tachometer, which was right in front of her on the dashboard, and was shocked to see that most of the time she was running at nearly seven thousand RPMs. Also, glancing at the speedometer, which went all the way up to 220 miles per hour, she saw that most of the time, she was running at nearly the top end of the speedometer. On one particular lap, she felt her birth sister Marta sitting with her. She glanced over and noticed Marta sitting in the other seat. *This is what you need, sister*, Marta told Dominika, *the love and support from your adopted family; and myself and our parents will always be with you.* Marta vanished after that, but Dominika started quietly crying tears of happiness. *I have so much love surrounding me*, she thought, *so I know that I can get through my trial.*

After about twenty hot laps, Dominika pulled Kenny into the pit area and climbed out. Her sisters all hugged and kissed her, along with her adopted parents. Then, it was time to reveal the lap times. Everyone was shocked to find that out of everyone's fastest lap ever on their home track here at the farm, Dominika was the fastest. Her fastest lap in Kenny had been even better then a record lap that Ken

Miles himself had set at LeMans in 1966 of three minutes and thirty point six seconds. Dominika's fastest lap time with Kenny had been three minutes and twenty nine point two seconds at two hundred-twenty two miles per hour. Tori and Ted then told the girls to head up to bed while they got Kenny back to the barn.

Once they'd all showered and changed into their pjs for the night, the girls all got together in a circle. Dominika asked her sisters why they were doing this.

"We want to tell you about our trials, Dominika," Barda announced.

"Yeah, so you can get some kind of idea of what we went through as a means of giving you some added strength," Kara added.

"You already know about mine," Dinah finished, "so Barda and Kara, go ahead and tell our sister about your trials."

CHAPTER 21

Barda began with her trial, which came about as a result of a ghost following her back to the farm. She, Dinah, and Kara had gone on a trip to an old mansion.

"Was it haunted, Barda," Dominika asked.

"There were a couple known ghosts, yes," Barda replied, "but the one that followed me back home wasn't from when it was a family home." She went on to explain that during the trip, she was able to sense the emotions of the resident ghosts, so they ended up having to leave early due to her gift as an empath. However, when they'd gotten home, Tori and Ted had noticed that Barda was still having these intense emotional moments, like she'd be perfectly fine one moment and the next moment she was crying her eyes out.

"Dad was the one who figured out that a ghost had followed me home," Barda explained, "and it was displaying it's emotions through me." Dominika asked how were they able to identify the ghost. Barda explained that they'd taken an ovilus, a digital dictionary that ghosts could use to speak, and a digital recorder, and placed them in the living room. Then, Ted sensed around and invited the ghost to come and communicate with them, and tell them why it had followed Barda home from the mansion. It hadn't taken long for the ghost to make itself known.

"It was the ghost of a teenage girl, named Veronica," Barda said, "and she was seeking help and closure."

"Why," Dominika asked.

"She'd been murdered at the mansion by a boyfriend," Kara answered, "and she wanted justice since the boyfriend hadn't been caught, arrested, and charged."

"Plus, her body had never been found either," Dinah added, "and she wanted a proper burial." Barda then told how the family had gone back to the mansion, and had told the staff who took care of the mansion what the situation was. Of course they had been stunned, but agreed to help search the grounds, along with the local police. With the ghost of Veronica using Ted's ability and Barda's, they were able to locate Veronica's body, which had been hastily buried in a shallow grave near one of the ponds. Then, they'd shown the police a sketch that Kara had made, with Ted directing her by channeling Veronica's spirit. What was shocking is that Barda had some of Veronica's looks, so when the police finally located where Veronica's former boyfriend lived, they had Barda go in to lure him out.

"Of course he thought I was Veronica, and said that I was supposed to be dead," Barda laughed, "and I told him that it shouldn't hurt at all if I kicked him in between the legs, which I did." He'd then taken off after her, yelling and cursing, but he ended up running right into the arms of the police, and he was arrested and found guilty of Veronica's murder.

"So, has she found peace," Dominika asked.

"Far as I know she has," Barda answered, "though I did hear that he has woken up screaming in the middle of the night by what he says is the ghost of the girlfriend he killed." The sisters all had a good laugh over this. Then Dominika asked Kara about her trial.

"It was quite scary," Kara said, "especially since my friend's soul was at stake."

"Her soul," Dominika asked, "how so?"

"My friend, Sandy, was nearly fully possessed by a demon, sis." When Kara said this, Dominika's face went pale, for she'd heard about demonic possession before, but hadn't really thought that it was something that was actually possible. Kara went on to explain that Sandy had suffered a loss when her brother died suddenly in a boating accident, and she'd been vulnerable.

"It was a few weeks later that myself and some of my other friends were noticing a change in Sandy," Kara continued.

"What kind of changes, sis," Dominika asked.

"Well, she didn't want to hang out, which is something she is always up for," Kara answered, "plus, she'd get these intense fits of rage, and superhuman strength." Kara even mentioned that Sandy had picked up and thrown a senior boy halfway across the school cafeteria one day.

"Oh my god," Dominika gasped.

"Yeah, we were there when that happened," Dinah added, "and we knew that wasn't the Sandy we knew and loved."

"Agreed," Barda chimed in, "I could sense that there was something else there with her, and I could feel that it wasn't good." They all went on to tell Dominika that they'd told Ted about what had been going on with Sandy, and learned that Ted told them that Sandy's brother was warning them that it was a demon that had attached itself to Sandy and was trying to possess her.

"Why did Kara have to rid Sandy of the demon," Dominika questioned.

"The reason is that I didn't want to lose my friend," Kara replied, "if the demon stayed, it would've fully possessed Sandy and my friend would've been gone forever." She went onto explain that she'd been able to explain to Sandy what was happening to her, which had been a massive relief for Sandy, but that was only the first step. Kara'd had to further tell her friend that if she was to rid herself of the demon, she had to want it gone, to want it to leave her alone.

"That was a little hard for her," Kara continued, "since she'd formed a bit of a bond with it, but she told it that she was done with it and that it had to leave her alone forever immediately."

"I-I'm guessing it didn't like that," Dominika stated, stuttering a little.

"Oh it was absolutely furious," Kara affirmed, "demons don't like being told what to do, especially being told they have to leave." Kara went on to tell that she'd had to restrain her friend, so that the demon wouldn't harm her. The demon had fought back, but in the end, it was no match for Kara. Kara successfully exorcised her friend and Sandy had been back to her normal, happy, bubbly self ever since.

"That is amazing, Kara," Dominika told her sister.

"Thanks, Dominika, though Dinah's trial was the most heart wrenching so far, particularly since we weren't sure she was going to survive the flight home."

"Yeah," Dinah responded, "I know I told you about my trial already, Dominika, but I should tell you about it in full detail." Dinah gave a little gulp, and sniffled slightly, just then.

"What's wrong, sister," Dominika asked.

"This is hard for me to talk about, Dominika," Dinah answered softly, "since it was indeed a very frightening time of my life, and as Kara said, I almost didn't survive." She explained that she and some of her friends decided to go on a spring break cruise a year ago. Dominika was a little shocked, but was even more surprised that her sisters' trials had all happened a year apart.

"When we first got on the ship, I could sense a lot of underlying sadness," Dinah continued, "plus it seemed like it was all from girls around our age."

"You were able to sense this because of your ability, right," Dominika asked.

"Exactly," Dinah confirmed. It was on the fourth night they were out at sea that she and her friends figured out it was all a trap. She told everyone that the crew of the ship all seemed evil and ominous, and her ability wasn't wrong.

"It was in the middle of the night when they grabbed us," she told her sisters, "they dragged us all to the heart of the ship and the captain chained a girl to this horribly ugly alter, recited a chant, and then stabbed every girl in the same places; her hands, her breasts, her butt, and between her legs." Dinah began to cry a little then, saying she could still hear the terrified wails and feel the pain and anguish every time she talked about her trial.

"However, there was something weird about how it went down," she said, once she'd regained control of her emotions, "they saved me for last." When Dominika asked why, all Dinah could guess was they could sense she had the ability to feel the emotions in the environment and that if they saved her for last, she'd be easier to sacrifice because she'd be so crushed and devastated.

"But they were wrong," Dominika asked.

"Yes, Dominika, they were wrong," Dinah confirmed, "*very* wrong." She explained that they all had a small bit of their father's psychic ability also, and the spirits of the dead girls were telling her how to free them in the time that the captain was sacrificing them.

"How did you do it," Dominika asked.

"I made the pressure in the boilers go too high," Dinah answered. It had been a nasty time after that, trying to get back up to the top of the ship and safely off.

"The captain and her minions fought really hard against me, but there were way more good spirits then bad ones, so they didn't stand a chance."

"When you say way more good spirits, you're referring to the spirits of the girls, right?"

"Yes." Dinah went on to say that even though the ship had started basically disintegrating and the evil captain and her minions did beat her up, she was able to set all the souls of those poor girls free, and make off with one of the ship's lifeboats.

"However, that wasn't the end of her ordeal, Dominika," Kara quietly said.

"Yes," Barda added, "it was just the first half." Dinah explained further that the emergency radio in the lifeboat was old and busted, and the rations were no good either. As she'd tried to make her way back to land, a massive storm had come through and thrown her into the water, where she'd gotten a really nasty bite on her left leg by a shark.

"Thankfully the shark chose not to hang on," Dinah sighed, "though I was bleeding pretty heavily." She said that she'd managed to make it back to the boat and was able to make it through the rest of the storm without being thrown overboard again. However, the next day, it was blazing hot.

"Since there was no sail or anything for me to cover myself with, I was getting roasted," she continued, "plus I was losing blood rapidly, even though I'd put a tourniquet on."

"Was it then that Barda, Kara, Mother, and Father went out to look for her in your old bomber," Dominika asked.

"It was," Dinah replied, "it was actually Dad who said we needed to get out there and find her." She explained that when she heard The Beast overhead, she thought at first it was her mind playing tricks on her, for she'd been in a lot of pain. However, when she'd looked up, she could see that it was indeed her family's old B-17.

"The only worrying thing was there was another storm coming," Dinah told everyone, "and it looked like a nasty one." Kara explained that they'd had to make several slow passes before Dinah had been able to get herself into the little cage, and then had barely any strength to hang on as they pulled her up.

"Once I was safely onboard," Dinah said, "Barda and Kara carried me back to the waist gunner's area near the tail." Kara explained that

Dinah passed out when they finally laid her gently on the floor, but she'd healed Dinah quickly.

"And that is why you don't have a scar," Dominika guessed.

"Actually I have a slight scar on me from the shark, Dominika," Dinah told her, "have yourself a look." She rolled the short leg of her sleep shorts up and showed Dominika two long, jagged faint lines on her upper thigh, which made Dominika gasp. However, she realized it was a battle scar, and her sister had won the battle.

"Thank you sisters for sharing the stories of your trials with me," she told them.

"Aww you're welcome, Dominika," Barda told her, "that's what sisters do." Then she, along with Kara and Dinah, all hugged Dominika.

"Don't fret too much, Dominika," Dinah said kindly, "we'll always be together and we'll always be with you."

"That is the truth right there," Kara added.

"We'd better get some sleep," Barda said, "we want our newest sister to earn her crown."

"Thank you again, sisters," Dominika sighed, "thank you." They then said their little chant and headed off to sleep, all hoping they were ready for the upcoming battle.

Meanwhile, Blohkin and his goons had readied themselves for battle. Blohkin was still fuming to himself that he and his friends hadn't been able to apprehend Dominika, or take care of her adopted parents. *Very very soon, Dominika Borov,* he thought, *you'll be back in the Rodina and in Sparrow School where you were meant to be, serving President Putin.* In his mind, once he and his friends captured Dominika, they'd torture her first, as a way of venting their frustration for all the trouble and humiliation she'd caused them before taking her back to Russia and handing her over to President Putin to be put into Sparrow training. However, they had no way of knowing that what actually would go down was anything but their full plan. Plus, Blohkin still didn't realize that his phone, which connected him directly to Putin, was still missing. Also, something that Putin *never* saw coming after the next day, would be ongoing terror from an ancient warrior princess as punishment for trying to control one of her descendants.

CHAPTER 22

SATURDAY DAWNED BRIGHT AND CLEAR like fresh spring water. Kara had dawn patrol, so while she was out Barda, Dinah, and Dominika gathered together along with their parents for breakfast. Just as they finished getting the table ready, Kara returned, saying all seemed quiet on the farm. Everyone seemed thankful, but they all knew that it was only the calm before the storm. Once Kara got seated at the table, they all said their morning prayers, adding the prayer to Saint Joan of Arc and to Saint Michael for extra help and protection.

"This is the day, Dominika," Barda said.

"Yes, Barda," Dominika replied, "but I'm still afraid."

"Afraid of what, Sis," Dinah asked.

"Something happening to all of you."

"I don't think that is anything to worry about," Ted told her.

"How and why is that, Father?"

"You've been training hard with your sisters, Dominika," Tori reminded, "plus you can tell what your opponent will do next with your ability to read minds."

"Yeah," Kara added, "plus, your movements are so swift and catlike, how could someone fighting you expect to win."

"Mother, Kara thank you," Dominika responded, blushing slightly. Ted also told his adopted daughter that when the light was hitting her red/brown hair, it looked like a perfectly aged red wine.

Her adopted mother and sisters all looked closely and agreed, which made Dominika blush harder, and made her giggle like the rest of the ladies in the family who giggled when they blushed. The family then went ahead and finished breakfast, clearing the table after.

As the girls were heading to the Workout House, Tori asked Dominika to stay back. Ted was a little stumped, but when he saw his wife look at him, he understood. Once Ted and her sisters were outside, Dominika had to ask Tori why she wanted to speak to her privately.

"Your adopted sisters told you about their trials last night, Honey" Tori explained, "however, there is one more trial you need to hear about."

"Whose is that, Mother," Dominika asked.

"Mine," Tori told her. Dominika gasped, but quickly understood that she should hear about her adopted mother's trial as well as those of her sisters.

"How was it, Mother," Dominika asked.

"It was one of the scariest nights of my life, Dominika," Tori responded. She went on to tell of how her wicked Aunt Stacy had hired a hitman to take care of Ted and then had chloroformed her into blacking out, only to wake up in a warehouse, naked and tied to an altar.

"Oh my god," Dominika gasped in horror, "so your aunt was going to sacrifice you!"

"She was, yes," Tori answered with a heavy shudder. However, she went on to say how just when her aunt was about to kill her, Ted had burst into the room and cut her free. This made Dominika swell with pride slightly, even though she tried to hide it. Tori explained that she and Ted had met on a train when she was eighteen and was moving from Queens, New York to Atlanta. She told her adopted daughter that back then, she wasn't as tough and brave as she was now. In fact, she'd been quite the opposite, scared and sad.

"What made you fall in love with Father," Dominika asked.

"He was the first person, other then my parents, who told me that my mismatched eyes were pretty," Tori explained. Dominika already knew that her adopted mother had mismatched eyes, and to her they were very pretty.

"Well, Father was right about your eyes, Mother," Dominika said, "they are pretty; plus they play nicely with your bright red hair."

"Thank you, Dominika," Tori replied with a little giggle, "Ted told me the same thing; however, what made me *really* fall in love with him was his love of classic cars, which I share." Tori continued on how Ted had told her that night how it was the spirits of her deceased parents that had told him to take her in, and that it was her aunt Stacy who'd done them in. When Dominika asked if Ted had confirmed that, she told her that he had by taking Bunny, the DeLorean, back to the dates of her parents' deaths. Plus, Tori told her adopted daughter of how earlier that evening, Ted had taken her to a dance at the local community center, which was the first dance that Tori had ever attended with a date.

"So that was your first date with Father then," Dominika asked.

"Yes, and it was the most magical night of my life," Tori replied, with her mismatched eyes sparkling at the memory, "plus, we shared our first kiss there, right after we were crowned the royal couple of the night." Tori point to some pictures on the wall near the staircase, and Dominika saw that it indeed was Tori and Ted at the dance.

"That leather dress you're wearing looks extremely sexy, Mother," Dominika said with a giggle.

"Yes, Ted thought so too," Tori confirmed, "though when I came downstairs and he gasped when he saw me, I did get a little nervous; however, it wasn't until after Ted and Bunny had gone back in time that night that I was scared just about out of my skin." She told Dominika that at first, she dreamt of her magical time with Ted at the dance, but then when they appeared to be dancing through the stars, a meteor struck Ted and he fell away from her and then she was consumed by darkness.

"Did you wake up then, Mother," Dominika asked.

"In my dream, which was fast becoming a nightmare, I did," Tori answered, shivering at the memory. Tori explained how she'd been tied tightly to an altar, naked, and that her wicked aunt was just about to stab her as a sacrifice when her eyes had flown open. Plus, it had been shortly after that that Ted and Bunny returned, and that he'd comforted her.

"I did fall asleep in his arms, but only after he took me to his room and gave me a gift," Tori continued.

"What was the gift, Mother," Dominika asked.

"Our ancestor, Xena's sword."

"You mean her actual sword, that she held in battle!?"

"Yes, Dominika." Continuing with her recount, Tori told Dominika that the next day was when they started training, and also it had been that evening at the local Pizza Hut that Ted confessed that he was indeed in love with her. Then, when she and Ted had gotten home, they'd had a few rounds of pool downstairs, and had snuggled on the couch for a showing of the movie **TITANIC**. Training resumed the next day and continued all up until Sunday.

"We'd gone to church and had decided to race when we got back here," Tori said, "then that is when it *really* began." She said that she heard a gunshot, and saw Ted fall, which made her feel like her heart had just been shattered inside her chest. She'd started to run towards him, but was struck in the side of the head by something heavy, and then was drugged into sleep by chloroform on a rag.

"Is that when realized your nightmare was coming true, Mother," Dominika asked, eyes getting wide.

"Yes, Honey," Tori said with a small muffled sob, followed by a hiccup, "I woke up and couldn't move and realized I was tied tightly to an altar naked, then Aunt Stacy appeared out of the darkness with a dagger; however just when she was about to sacrifice me, Ted burst in to save me." She told of how Ted had quickly cut her free and told her evil aunt that he'd fallen in love with her. She and Ted had gotten out and back to the farm, but that had only been the beginning. Ted then gave Tori Xena's actual battle clothes and when she'd put on her ancestor's clothes and weapons, her strength, courage, and love increased.

"We then went out onto the little balcony and shared a kiss, and talked to each other," Tori explained, "and it was shortly after that that my aunt and her hitman arrived." Ted had then taken on her aunt's hitman, Chad Peterson, in a ten second drag race, which Ted won, and then Tori took on her aunt in a Japanese Drift race, which Tori won. However, Stacy and her hitman felt that it hadn't been fair, so they came back to the farm and had a mixed tag team wrestling match in the Workout House. Ted had gotten Chad to submission, and then Tori had gotten her aunt to submit also.

"Though Chad did try and attack Ted after I beat my aunt," Tori went on, "but Ted put him out with a 'Tombstone Piledriver', which I think is the scariest wrestling move I've ever heard of or seen."

"What about your aunt, Mother," Dominika asked. Tori said that Ted pointed out how her aunt was escaping, and that in that moment she'd been filled with a burning, raging anger and had taken off after her. Once she'd brought her aunt to a stop, she had fought her aunt, and triumphed. However, Tori had suffered some wounds and right after her aunt was defeated forever, her wounds had erupted into intense pain and she'd passed out from it.

"Ted found me then, and kissed me," Tori said, with happy tears coming into her eyes, "I revived, and my wounds were healed." Also, she told of how her parents made themselves visible to her and Ted and then that the spirit of Xena appeared also and named her as the modern Warrior Queen.

"What happened after that," Dominika asked. Tori concluded the story of her trial by telling her adopted daughter that after she and Ted had gotten back to the farm and stashed the cars, he'd taken her down by the creek and proposed to her right there under the moonlight.

"Of course, I said 'yes'," Tori finished, "and the rest is history."

"That's such a wonderful ending, Mother," Dominika sighed.

"It is, *Dushka*; now best get over to the Workout House and join your sisters." As Dominika raced out to the Workout House, Tori headed upstairs to the main bedroom she and Ted shared. She sat on the bed and went into meditation, trying to see what the outcome of her adopted daughter's trial might be. However, all she kept seeing was mainly her, Ted, Barda, Dinah, and Kara dying at the hands of Blohkin and his goons. This greatly saddened Tori, for she didn't want to have to tell Ted this. Towards the end of her meditation, though, she saw a bright white light flash and then herself, Ted, and their daughters all alive and well at the farm, which was very confusing. *How do we die, but then come back to life*, she wondered, *and what happens to Dominika between the time we all die and then resurrect?* Tori still pondered this as she took her ancestor's sword out of the closet and began to polish it.

Meanwhile, Ted was putting the girls through their paces. It truly was amazing to see Dominika taking to their style of fighting so quickly, but he had to remind himself that she was blood related to them, so it wasn't all that odd. When it was time for everyone to take a breather, he asked Dominika how she was feeling.

"I feel good, Father," she said, "however, I'm still nervous."

"What are you nervous about, *Dushka*," Ted asked.

"I-I don't want anything to happen you and Mother, or my sisters," Dominika replied, as the tears started falling out of her aquamarine/sapphire eyes, "I've already lost my family once, and I just don't want to have to go through that again." Ted hugged his adopted daughter and soon was joined by Dinah, Barda, and Kara. As she was hugged by her adopted family, Dominika felt her tears subsiding, and her strength return. However, just as they pulled apart, Tori came running in, all out of breath. Ted immediately had a hunch she'd seen something.

"What is it, Honey," he asked his wife.

"That Blohkin guy and his goons," Tori gasped in between breaths, "they'll be arriving here after dark." This made everyone gasp, though Dominika was the only one who let out a frightened yelp.

"We need a plan of attack," Barda said.

"Yeah, but what," Kara asked.

"I think I have an idea for that, girls," Ted answered, "come over here and let me show y'all a map of our property." After pulling a map of their property out, Ted showed how Tori could have Super Tank, their fully functional, supercharged, Sherman Tank, closing off the main entrance, and then he could use the Ripsaw, the small attack tank from **<u>FATE OF THE FURIOUS</u>** and then the girls could use the off road cars to surround their enemy.

"Know your enemy like the land you fight on, right Dad," Dinah asked.

"Exactly, Honey," Ted replied.

"Plus this gives us another advantage," Kara realized.

"What is that, Sis," Dominika asked.

"If the enemy has you out manned and out gunned, that is the time to out think them," Kara answered.

"Well then we'd better practice," Tori told them all, "so that we're ready for tonight." For the rest of the afternoon, the Crystals practiced everything, from their hand to hand combat skills to their vehicle attack formations. When the it got around evening, they all headed inside for a quick meal, and to prepare. They had a healthy size steak and potatoes, along with a few small Russian side dishes, which greatly pleased Dominika. Once they'd finished eating and the table had been cleared, they all headed upstairs to their rooms. As Dominika put on her Warrior Princess attire, she felt a presence. She turned and gasped, for she saw her ancestor Xena standing in her room again.

"It is time, my descendant," Xena told her, "to face your trial, just like your adopted mother and sisters."

"Will I be able to survive, as well as my adopted family," Dominika asked.

"That cannot be said."

"Why?!"

"Somethings are meant to be told to you, dear girl; others must come about by way of natural causes."

"I don't want to be an orphan, nor do I want to go back to Russia, for if I do, I'll become a sex slave to Putin."

"I will tell you that nothing of that sort will happen to you, but that is all I can, and will, tell you." With that, Xena started fading.

"Wait," Dominika screamed, but her ancestor had vanished. Just then, her sisters came into her room.

"What's wrong, Dominika," asked Dinah, "we heard you scream just now."

"Xena came and spoke to me again, sisters," Dominika confessed. That was all she was able to get out before she began to cry. Barda, Dinah, and Kara all hugged their adopted sister until her tears stopped. Shortly after this, Tori and Ted came in. They asked their daughters if they were ready, and the girls all said they were. The whole family then gathered in a circle and held hands and said a prayer together. After they prayed, they gathered their weapons and headed for the garage.

Tori and Ted got their two tanks fired up and headed out to their positions. Meanwhile the girls got their off road cars fired up and headed to their positions. As Dominika waited with Dirt Devil, she did the usual radio check with everyone, which went well with everyone being able to hear each other loud and clear. *This is it,* she thought, *my trial has begun.* Little did she know it would be a frightening experience for her. Also, she had no way of knowing that she would become the strongest of all her sisters, but also be able to exact some revenge on the Russian leader from right on American soil.

Dominika just focused on trying to keep her courage strong. Pretty soon, she heard over the CB that there were cars coming onto their property and they weren't friendly ones. *Alright, here we go,* she said to herself, *time to go from a damsel in distress to a warrior princess.*

CHAPTER 23

Blohkin and his friends pulled their cars into Old Muscle Farm, killed the engines, emerged with their weapons ready. They'd only taken a few steps when there was a loud boom and one of their vehicles exploded. Suddenly a Sherman tank charged out of the brush straight towards them, weapons going. As they dived for cover, there was suddenly a smaller boom and another of their cars exploded. Turning they saw a smaller attack tank race out of the brush on the side their backs were facing.

"Holy smokes," one of Blohkin's buddies exclaimed, "I thought this was just a farming family; I didn't think they owned a couple of operational tanks." As they continued to engage the tanks, they heard loud engines coming from out of the brush on multiple sides. Looking around, they saw several cars, modified for off road, race out into the barnyard. They saw that one was a modern Dodge Challenger, another was a 1969 Chevrolet Camaro, still another an all terrain armored fighter. However the one they seemed amazed at was the one that turned out to be a 1970 Dodge Charger. Pretty soon, Blohkin and his friends were completely out of ammunition and three of their four cars had been destroyed. Plus, they were now surrounded by the four modified cars and the two tanks. Slowly five hooded figures emerged, one from each tank and one from three of the modified cars. Also, Blohkin and his friends saw that the figures were armed.

"Who are all of you," Blohkin bellowed. The figures slowly lowered their hoods and said their names, one by one.

"Tori Crystal," she growled.

"Ted Crystal," he roared.

"Barda Crystal," she yelled.

"Dinah Crystal," she screeched.

"Kara Crystal," she hollered.

"Then who is in that modified Charger," one of Blohkin's goons asked. The figure in the Charger slowly rose from the car via the roof hatch and lowered it's hood, making Blohkin and his friends gasp in shock.

"Dominika Crystal," she bellowed, "I belong to this family now, so you have no right to be here." Then, Tori let out their battle cry and the whole family leaped into action. The Russian government agents were really surprised with how the family was able to fight, especially since they weren't using guns but rather ninja weapons.

As the battle raged on, Dominika fought with everything she had. She and her adopted family were able to fight off the goons quite well, but Blohkin was proving to be maybe more then they could handle. When Dominika was fighting with two of Blohkin's friends, she heard Ted yell in pain and then shortly after heard Tori along with her adopted sisters screaming. It was here that she faltered, turning to see where they were. This led to her being grabbed from behind and promptly knocked out cold.

Blohkin stood over Dominika's limp body. All of his friends were dead, but that was alright since they were expendable anyway. He also looked over at her adopted family, who were all dead too. *Now she has nobody,* he thought proudly to himself, *I'll hold her in the old house I saw on the drive out here and give her Russian prison treatment before flying us back to Moscow.* He stripped Dominika naked, wrapped her limp body in a long cloth, dumped her in the trunk of the one remaining car he and his team had brought, and headed for the old abandoned cottage he'd seen on the way to the farm. Little did he know that Dominika *still* wouldn't be going back to Russia, and that Blohkin would never see Russia again either.

CHAPTER 24

AFTER WHAT SEEMED LIKE FOREVER, Dominika awoke. She was sitting on the floor in a dimly lit room and found her arms and legs hurting really bad. Also, she was horrified to find that she was completely naked. Plus she felt very cold. Suddenly, a wave of freezing cold water poured over head, and she let out a scream. When she did so, a hard hand whacked her in the back of the head, followed by another wave of freezing cold water getting poured over her head, making her scream again. Once she got hold of herself again, she heard a familiar nasty voice speak.

"Welcome to your little prison," Blohkin said with a nasty laugh, "this is what you get for upsetting the president." He then bent down in front of her, grabbed her chin hard and forced her to look at him.

"Are you ready to going home and beginning your life as a Sparrow?" He let her chin go so that she could answer.

"I'll *never* become a Sparrow, you sick bastard," Dominika spat, "**Never!**" Blohkin responded by slapping her hard on the cheek.

"Either you return to Russia and become a Sparrow for President Putin, or die in this basement, Little Miss Tits," he snarled. He then took out a small tazer and put it in between Dominika's legs. He then zapped her with it, which made her scream again. Once that was over, he had fun with her breasts, however it was only fun for him. To Dominika, she felt like her breasts were being murdered, for he was squeezing them so hard and pulling on her nipples so hard also, that after a bit, she could hardly speak from screaming in agony so much.

After torturing Dominika for nearly another full hour, Blohkin left to use the phone. Dominika decided to meditate to try and make contact with her family. As she closed her eyes, she felt herself slipping out of consciousness. *No, no,* she screamed to herself in a panic, *you can't fall out of it now; you can't!* However, her mind and body were so fatigued from her fighting as well as the Russian prison treatments Blohkin had inflicted upon her that she quickly slipped into unconsciousness.

Dominika awoke in a strange place. There were stars and swirls all around, yet there also seemed to be no solid ground and she found herself standing on some sort of invisible solid. As she continued to look around and wonder where she was, she heard a familiar voice say her name.

"Dominika." She whipped around and saw Xena standing behind her. Dominika was so overwhelmed with emotion that all she could really do was run into Xena's arms and cry.

"I'm so sorry," she sobbed, "I've failed you, and my trial; now I'll never see my adopted family ever again." However, she felt her ancestor quietly shushing her, which made her calm down quickly. Looking up, she saw that Xena was smiling at her in a warm way.

"You haven't failed me or your trial, my descendant," Xena told her softly, "plus your adopted family isn't really dead, but rather unconscious; also you've gained all their abilities."

"I have," Dominika asked. However, she realized that as she was asking that question, she found it was a stupid question, for she remembered feeling new things rushing into her when she'd been battling back at the farm.

"Also, your trial isn't over," Xena continued, "it is only just begun." She explained to Dominika that Blohkin was in truth a demon from her nightmares that had been haunting her ever since her mother had died.

"Your mother knew this, but she didn't want to tell you," Xena explained further, "since that would've made you even more frightened and given him added strength." Just then Dominika saw people appearing behind Xena. Xena stood aside and Dominika saw both her birth family and her adopted family approaching. All of them hugged her, and began giving her words of encouragement.

"You can do this, sister," Marta told her, giving her a big hug.

"This is your last battle before you can truly be free, Honey," her mother Irina said comfortingly.

"You're prepared for this, Dominika," Ted said confidently.

"You've got all the weapons you need," Tori assured her.

"Now **FIGHT**," her adopted sisters said as one. With that, they all vanished, leaving her alone with Xena again. When she looked down at herself, Dominika saw she was again wearing her Warrior Princess garb. Xena then stepped up to her.

"You will see your adopted family again soon, my descendant," she told her again, "however, there is one more thing you need, and that is something from me." At this, Xena drew her sword and handed it to Dominika. Dominika was shocked, since Xena's sword was with her adopted mother the last time she'd seen it, but she bowed before her ancestor and accepted the weapon. As she stood up, Xena hugged her and whispered, "Now, my descendant, it is time for your trial to actually begin; slay your demon." Once that was said, Dominika's world went dark again.

CHAPTER 25

⎯⎯⎯⎯⎯⎯⎯⎯

ALL AT ONCE, DOMINKA WAS awake and freed of her chains. Plus she was wearing her Warrior Princess outfit, and had Xena's sword in her hands. So, when Blohkin came into the room, he was shocked, but it only lasted a moment and he showed himself as he truly was: a horrifying demon that seemed straight out of her worst nightmare.

"Now, you pathetic girl," it said, "prepare to face my wrath and then the wrath of the modern Tsar." However, Dominika had closed her eyes and was focusing her energy and strength. As she did this, she heard the voices of her adopted family in her mind encouraging her, as well as the words of her and her adopted sisters' fight song, 'Roar' by Katy Perry. As the demon continued to hurl insults and threats her way, she felt her courage and anger increasing. Finally, she let out a loud roar that literally forced the demon silent. At this Dominika attacked with the same battle cry her mother had hollered at the farm.

As she battled the demon, she kept listening to her ancestor's words and the words of her adopted family in her head. Plus she used everything she'd learned during her training, and to her surprise it was working. Also, after a while, a tiara appeared on her head.

"What's up with the crown," the demon demanded.

"It is proof of what I am, you pathetic creature," Dominika growled.

"And what are you, a pageant queen?"

"I'm a Warrior Princess, and I shall defeat you." With that Dominika kept demonstrating the fruits of her training to her foe.

Finally, she got the demon in a corner, right where she wanted it.

"Do you know what happens in a battle between love and hate," she snarled at the demon.

"W-what," it croaked.

"Love always wins." At that, Dominika's sword started glowing with a bright white light, a pure, warm white light and she stabbed the demon directly in the chest. With a final piercing screech it vanished. As it did, Dominika's Warrior Princess outfit vanished, as did her sword and she collapsed on her back.

"Everyone, thank you," she whispered softly before passing out.

Eventually, Dominika awoke in a hospital room. As she looked about, she noticed the sheriff CJ Jones sitting in the corner. When she went to sit up, she groaned a little with the effort and the sheriff came over and helped her.

"I'm glad to see that you're awake, Dominika," CJ told her, "I was a little worried."

"How long have I been here," she croaked.

"Nearly a week," the sheriff answered, "when the EMTs found you passed out at that old house a few miles away from the farm, you were so weak that they weren't sure if you'd wake up." The sheriff then went on to explain how the hospital folks were so surprised that she'd actually recovered from what happened at the old house, and that they were saying it was nothing short of a miracle.

"However, you are getting released today," he continued, "so that it is why I'm here."

"Am I going to live with you, Mr. Jones," Dominika asked nervously, feeling her throat starting to tighten and her heart starting to hurt.

"Ha ha, no I'm just here to help you get on your feet and out the door," CJ told her with a hearty laugh, "the people you are going home with are waiting for you in the lobby; and I do believe you'll be happier then a pig in mud when you see them." Dominika tried to get the sheriff to say who it was she'd be going home with, but he wouldn't say anything more. After getting dressed and with the sheriff walking beside her, Dominika headed for the lobby of the hospital. However, before she actually got there, she noticed who it was: her adopted family, Tori, Ted, Barda, Kara, and Dinah. They were all standing there, alive and well, with huge smiles on their faces.

Her shriek of shock was so loud that it brought many people running to see what the emergency was. Plus, her shock in general was so great at that moment that it made her fall to her knees. However, Dominika quickly got back on her feet and ran into the open arms of her adopted family as happy tears streamed out of her sapphire/aquamarine eyes in torrents.

"I love you all so much," Dominika sobbed.

"We love you too, sister," Barda, Dinah, and Kara said at the same time.

"We love you very much also, Princess," Tori and Ted told her. After a few more minutes of hugs and happy tears, the Crystals headed out to where the General Lee was waiting. The girls climbed into the back while Tori and Ted got in the front, through the windows naturally. As they headed back to the farm, Ted told Dominika that he'd managed to snatch something of Blohkin's when he and his goons had first tried to attack the farm.

"What is it, Father," she asked.

"His phone, with a direct connection to the Russian leader," Ted replied, "I thought it would be good for all of us to give the bastard a call and tell him he's going to have to cancel his plans for you to go to State School Four." At this, Dominika squealed loudly with joy, and her sisters joined in as well with a few whoops.

"Before all that can happen, there is something more important that must happen first," Tori announced.

"What is that, Mother," Dominika asked.

"Your crowning, sis," Barda told her.

"My what," Dominika gasped.

"Your crowning, Dominika," Kara repeated.

"Where you finally get your Warrior Princess tiara," Dinah added, "just like the rest of us." Dominika was so happy in that moment, her eyes just exploded with happy tears all over again. Of course her face turned red as well, which made her start laughing through her tears. Her sisters started laughing with her and hugged her tight.

When they finally got back to the farm and had gotten the General parked back in his stall, they all gathered on the drag strip for Dominika's crowning, just as they'd done for when Barda, Dinah, and Kara had earned their Warrior Princess titles. Ted walked Dominika up to Tori, Barda, Dinah, and Kara. Kissing her hand, he gave her a big, warm smile and then a gentle little nudge forward. Stepping up to her adopted mother and adopted sisters, Dominika bowed. Barda then handed Dominika her sword, Kara her shakrom, and Dinah her breast dagger. Finally, Tori placed Dominika's Warrior Princess crown on her head and helped her adopted daughter to her feet.

"Thank you, all of you," Dominika said through a few happy tears, "thank you so much."

"You're more then welcome, Honey," Tori told her. At that, they all embraced their adopted family member, related to them by blood and now through tradition: Dominika Crystal. After Dominika's crowning ceremony, they decided to give the Russian leader a call.

After a few rings, Putin's face appeared on the screen, and he saw Dominika.

"Ahh, Ms. Borov," he said smoothly, "I take that Mr. Blohkin has you comfortable and ready for your trip back to the motherland."

"Blohkin is dead, you slime," Dominika snarled, "also Dominika Borov is dead too."

"How is Blohkin dead," the Russian leader wondered out loud, "and that is no way to talk to your leader."

"I killed him," Dominika growled, "and I don't belong to Russia, or you, anymore." Putin still refused to believe what he was hearing and kept on insisting that Dominika return to Moscow and report to State School Four immediately upon her arrival.

"I don't have to, you sick bastard," she retorted, "besides, I'm royalty now, along with my adopted family."

"Royalty, how," Putin exclaimed, "and what do you mean about an adopted family?" At that, Dominika's entire adopted family came into the picture, plus Xena appeared as well.

"This is my family now, you slimy snake," Dominika told him with a growl, "and I'm also now a citizen of the United States of America." Then Ted asked the Russian leader if the letters 'f' and 'o' meant anything to him. Finally, while Putin was still throwing a fit, they all drew their swords and stabbed them into the screen at the same time. Little did they know that this would result in something strange occurring to Putin. Literally that night, and every night thereafter, Putin was visited by Xena and she tormented him, his military, and everything he'd done to Russia and the world until Putin was going mad with anger and craziness.

After destroying Blohkin's phone and throwing its remains in the trash, the Crystals knew they should get to practicing for the twenty four hour race coming up. Dominika and Kara were the two who would be driving Ken Miles' Ford GT40 and knew that Kara had yet to get familiar with the old Ford so they headed for the barn to get it.

A few hours later, the Crystals were still at it. Dominika and Kara were now very familiar with the old GT40 and were turning out lap times so fast that Ted remarked that it would've made Ken Miles himself green with envy. Plus, Ted, Tori, Barda, and Dinah were an incredible pit crew, especially considering the GT40 has single center lugs on all four tires and you have to use a rubber mallet and bang on them to get them loose and then bang on them to tighten them up, and also jacking up a car that is literally only forty inches tall is hard work too. However, pit stop times were like only two and a half to three minutes usually, which is very good for a team using a small pit crew and an older car.

However, after they'd finished practicing for the evening and had gotten the GT40 back in it's stall, Dominika told her adopted family that when she was driving it, she felt the same way she did when she and her sisters were on the trail between the shop and home: wild and free.

"That's how you're supposed to feel, sis," Dinah told her. Soon they were all sitting around the fire pit down by the creek. After discussing everything in order to get ready for the upcoming race, Dominika suggested to her sisters that they sing to their parents.

"I think that is a good idea," Tori approved.

"I know just the song," Dominika announced, "ready, sisters?"

"Ready, sister," Barda, Kara, and Dinah said as one. They then sang their fight song. When they got to where they all would roar, they ended up roaring so loud that it reverberated off the trees and stones in the area. Once the song was over, they extinguished the fire and headed off to bed. However, the girls gathered in Dominika's room in their circle. They asked God to give them strength and courage for the week ahead and to watch over them forever. Also, they asked for his protection on Dominika and Kara in the upcoming race. Once their prayers were over, and before turning in for the night, they gave their little chant: "Warrior Princesses now, Warrior Queens forever."

EPILOGUE

The first annual 24 Hours of Covington auto race had concluded and it was a total shock to everyone that the Crystals ended up winning since they had the oldest car in the line up. However, it wasn't too terribly surprising when the other competitors and the spectators saw that it was truly the second place car from the 1966 24 Hours of Le Mans. Ted, Tori, Barda, and Dinah had worked hard and tirelessly to keep the old GT40 going, and Dominika and Kara had driven it hard, fast, and effortlessly. When they were up on the victory podium, Dominika was asked if she'd like to say a few words. After blushing a little, she began her speech.

"This win does mean a lot to me, and even more for my family. You see, the Crystals adopted me and made me a part of their family. However, even though I am an adopted member of the family, I am actually blood related to them in a very distant way. It was my sisters here who brought me home, in the trunk of our number one car, the General Lee, and then found me nearly dead in the trunk. I'd escaped to this country with my birth sister, Marta, but she sadly was murdered right before my eyes. Before she was killed, however, she told me to save myself, and that is what I did. Her killer chased after me, even shot me in the leg, but I kept going. I ended up falling and hitting my head on a rock. When I came to, I dragged myself through the woods until I saw the General parked by a pond where my adopted sisters were picnicking. When they got back to the farm, they found me in the trunk and I was nearly dead. However, they helped me heal and quickly took me into their care and raised me as one of their own. As I trained with them, I felt like I somehow was connected to them, and it turns out that I am. An ancestry search proved it. When it came time for me to face the man who killed my birth sister, I was still scared at first. However, thanks to my training with my adopted family here, I was able to triumph over him. Now, I share the same last name as my family, Crystal. Also, if it weren't for Ted, Tori, Dinah, and Barda's hard work in the pits, Kara and myself wouldn't have been able to finish this race the way we did. So I thank all of you for allowing myself and my family to be a part of this and for coming out to support this wonderful town." After her speech, Ted was asked to say a few words and he reflected on how amazing it was to watch two of his daughters in the race, and to give Ken Miles a victory, in a way. Plus, he touched on what he felt the GT40 stood for: a symbol of what the American auto industry can do if it puts it's mind to achieving a goal, and showing the world what an American car is capable of.

Once all the other speeches were concluded, the Crystals were presented with the big trophy and photographed. As they were loading up Kenny, which was the name they'd given the GT40 in honor of Ken Miles, one of the photographers came over and told them that there seemed to be more people on the victory podium then just the six of them. Looking at the photos, they all saw Dominika's birth family as well as Xena standing with them. However, the Crystals just laughed and said that maybe some ghosts photo bombed the shot, but that they should stay and not be edited out.

When they got back to the farm, Dominika and the girls decided to take out some of the exotics and race them. So, Dominika picked out the Bugatti Divo, Barda chose the Lamborghini Aventador, Dinah chose the McLaren F1, and Kara selected the Ferrari Enzo. So, with Ted manning the stopwatches and Tori acting as flagger they took off from the starting line. The girls had car to car communication in their helmets so they all talked and joked as they flew around their home track at the farm. However, all of them knew that they were all together because of love; their love for cars but most importantly their love for each other. And if they kept loving each other in the way they always have, there is nothing that can destroy them. Safe to say, with all the love that the Crystals have for themselves and their huge collection of cars, they all lived happily, and speedily, ever after.

THE END